surAvani

By Alexandra Vrba

Printed in the United States of America

First Printing, 2017Photo rights reserved

Cover Design reserved

Content reserved

Publisher: BookBaby

E-book Distribution on: iBookstore, Amazon Kindle, Barnes & Noble, Kobo, Baker &
Taylor, Copia, Gardners, eSentral, Scribd, Goodreads, Oyster, Flipkart, Ciando, Vearsa

Print ISBN: 978-1-54390-615-8

eBook ISBN: 978-1-54390-616-5

This book is dedicated to the many friends and family who believed in me and encouraged me. Thank you for your never ending love and support.

Special thanks to:

My editor - Karen C. Armstrong
Karen I cannot thank you enough for helping me make my novel the best that it could be, and in turn, making me a better writer.

Photo - Thank you to my wonderful photographer Robin at Robin Blankenship Photography for capturing exactly what I had imagined.

Cover Design - Myiah Bethel, thank you for being so easy to work with and changing the cover a hundred times until I was happy.

Cover Model - Elizabeth Baldwin, you are beautiful. Thank you for being my surAvani!

CHAPTER 1
-Andie-

I REMEMBER MY TENTH BIRTHDAY. I DON'T REMEMBER THE theme, or the cake, or the presents I got, but I do remember my parents and the other adults talking. Even as a kid I noticed the excitement in some voices and the fear in others; the whispers and the nervous glances. I remember overhearing my father listen to the news while I ate my Cheerios that morning. "It has been confirmed, by numerous scientists, paranormal experts, geneticists, and even the President of the United States, that several supernatural species believed to be nothing more than myths, are in fact thriving and living right here in our communities. Early this morning, werewolves, witches, and vampires all announced to the world that they do in fact exist."

"What a load of crap" my father said as he switched off the T.V.

By the afternoon, when the other kids started arriving for my party, more stories were being passed around. There were videos on the internet of people changing into wolves – 'shifting' they called it; of vampires jumping to incredible heights and moving at impossible speeds, and witches doing magic for the camera. Nothing dangerous of course, according to one witch interviewed for the news "they didn't want to scare us, just prove that they existed." My tenth birthday was the last birthday party I ever had.

By the time I was twelve, the humans in the world had come to accept the fact that these creatures lived amongst us. Those first few years weren't so bad, the supernatural kept a pretty low profile. Every once in a while you would hear that a small group of people went missing, or a random nobody had been found slaughtered and ripped to shreds but no one ever made a big fuss, and the occurrences were soon forgotten.

When I was thirteen it became the new fad, like tattoos or piercings. You could sign up to become one of them. Anyone could be a "Donor": people who volunteer to let the vampires feed on them. Most of them are usually treated well. Food, money, amazing vampire sex… but it comes with the high risk of dying from too much blood loss. The vamps can't always control themselves, especially the new ones. It was harder to actually become one. Most of the vampires were willing to change a human, but they were conceded, and only willing to change those they thought worthy. The Werewolves were more selective, not out of arrogance, but more because they wanted each human they changed to really consider what would happen to them after they were bitten. Most of the witches stayed out of it. They were willing to let the world know they existed, and some of them would perform small spells or charms for a fee, but they never advertised for recruitment. I suppose that's because you have to be born a witch, you can't just ask to be changed into one.

By my fifteenth birthday, humans had become the minority. My mother left us to become a Donor with the hope that one day the vampire she served would be willing to change her. For her, the chance at immortality was worth giving up her life and family. My father shot himself shortly after learning of her death. I was left alone. I still had Rory; he had been my best friend since before I could remember. But it wasn't the same as having my parents, try as Rory might to fill the gap.

The way of life began to shift again. Not slowly like before, but in a matter of months. Most of the world's governments dissolved; countries were disbanded, and the land was broken up into territories. Each territory was ruled by a single pack or coven, and it didn't take long before wars for territory began breaking out. Soon every species was fighting each other out in the open, and before long, the human race had begun to disappear completely.

Now, at the ripe old age of nineteen, I live on the outskirts of society with a small group of humans Rory and I found while on the run from a wolf pack that had caught our scent in their territory. While werewolves aren't typically aggressive towards humans, they are very territorial, and if provoked can be extremely dangerous.

Our group travels, never staying in one place for more than a few nights. We all take turns keeping watch since more often than not, we are illegally camping on someone's territory. It's not the best, but it's more protection and support than we had before. I actually started to feel at home again. Little did I know the world was getting ready to drop out from under my feet one more time.

CHAPTER 2

"Hey Andie!" I hate my nickname. My mother always called me by my full name, Cassandra, but my father always wanted a boy, so he called me Andie for short, and the name stuck. "Andie!" It was Rory calling. I came out of our tent and headed towards the middle of camp. The last few days had been rough. The rain hadn't stopped for three days straight and our camp looked more like tents floating in a swamp than an actual camp. Most of the others had begun to pack up; we were near the edge of a werewolf territory, and we knew that after three days of heavy rains the wolves would be out enjoying the sun. We needed to move. There were four others gathered around the middle of camp, including Rory. Andre, our leader, and his son and second-in-command Stephen were also there.

"What's going on? Why aren't you busy packing?" I asked as I stepped closer.

They all gave me a look. "We need to make a run," said Stephen.

"A run? Are you crazy?! The area will be crawling with wolves soon; we need to get moving." Another look passed around the circle. Andre was old school military and had a habit of keeping the men in charge. As a result, as one of the few females in camp, I seemed to be left out of the 'need to know' group more often than not.

"What's wrong?" It was a statement, not a question. Rory looked at me.

"The supply tent flooded last night. We lost most of our supplies."

"How much is most?"

"A little more than half." It was Andre who spoke this time. "You are our fastest runner, Andie. And our next campsite is in the opposite direction of the nearest town." I sighed to myself. It was true. I was our fastest runner. I always loved running as a kid, but I never thought it would become key to my survival.

"When do we leave?" I asked.

"Five minutes. You, Stephen, and AJ will make the run, and rendez-vous back with the rest of the group at the new campsite. Stephen knows where it's at."

"I'm going on the supply run too," said Rory.

"Sorry Rory, you would be of more use helping to pack up the rest of camp rather than out on that run." Rory looked put out, but he knew Andre's word was final. AJ was an ok runner, but he was strong, which meant he could carry a lot. As second-in-command, Stephen was not only our guide, but he was almost as fast at running as I was. But Rory, sweet Rory, was clumsy and slow. A small smile crossed my lips as I remembered us freshman year: him trying to keep up with me the one and only time he decided to join me for my morning run. The moment down memory lane didn't last long. "I'll make a quick list of the things we need most, and then you need to go." Andre stated before walked away.

Stephen looked at me. "Race you there?" I smiled again in response to his question. Rory looked hurt. We had tried dating at one point, but it didn't work. Shortly after I lost both my parents, Rory tried to step into the boyfriend role. He became even more protective than usual with me, which irritated me, and just made me act out even more. We ended the dating so we didn't have to end our friendship, but Rory never quite lost the feelings he had for me. The way Stephen and I sometimes flirted made him uncomfortable and so he walked away, mumbling something about helping to pack as he went.

I used the thick tie I had around my wrist to pull my hair up into a ponytail and stretched for a moment while we waited for Andre to return with the list. It didn't take him long, and once we were ready we set out at a steady pace.

CHAPTER 3

TWENTY MINUTES LATER, SWEATY AND PANTING, WE SLOWED as we came to the edge of town. Once the government went down, most businesses closed. The bars were really the only places still operating and making a profit; vampires and werewolves can drink liquor, a lot of liquor. The grocery and retail stores were a hit or miss. There were a select few, run by werewolves, that were known to trade with humans, but they were few and far between. The rest of the time the stores were usually locked up, to be opened only when the leader of the territory needed something. The few humans left usually ended up breaking and entering, taking only what they needed before leaving, but it's a risky venture since it usually requires going right into the middle of a territory, where you risk being seen and taken. Humans are now a rare commodity. Those surviving do their best to stay well hidden because vampires are known to pay well to have you as a slave and eventually turn you into a willing Donor.

The grocery was thankfully closer to the edge of town than the middle. Though locked up to prevent looters like us, it appeared empty; and there are ways to get around a dead bolt. We edged our way around, sticking close to shadows and crouching behind abandoned cars and other cover. The unlucky part? We were upwind of the store. That small fact made me on edge.

Both vampires and werewolves have incredible senses of smell. Most vampires wont risk the sun, it burns them to ashes if they stay in the sunlight. But if they don't have to go far, they can move quickly enough that not much damage is done while they move, and they heal unbelievably fast, only slightly faster than the wolves do. Vampires are pretty easy to spot as well. With their porcelain white skin and flawless features, they don't blend in very well next to humans. Wolves are trickier to spot. They can change at will, and you may not know you're standing face to face with one until they do change. The signs are subtle, but they are there. Their eyes glow in the right light, or if their emotions are running high, even in human form, almost like a true wolf in the wild. Something they used to hide with contact lenses. The canines are slightly longer and more pronounced than a normal humans as well.

Getting into the store was no problem. Stephen was very good at picking locks and we decided to split the list and get things done faster. I took the canned foods aisle. Canned veggies, canned meat, canned beans. They all had a long shelf life. On my way back I passed through the bakery hoping to grab some stale bread. To my dismay, the bread was gone. I heard AJ shout, and then a large crash coming from the other side of the store. I froze long enough for my heart to beat twice, and then made a silent dash behind the counter of the bakery. I crouched there, hand covering my mouth, trying to quiet and slow my breathing. The hairs on the back of my neck stood up and I slowly turned. Across from me, hiding behind the deli side of the counter, sat a girl. We stared at one another. She looked horrible. Her pale and dirty cheeks had tear streaks running down them. She mouthed something at me, the single word "Please" forming on her lips before she pressed a finger to them.

I nodded. I wasn't sure where she came from, but I wasn't inclined to be making any noise. She seemed reassured for a brief moment before a look of horror came across her pale features. "Izzy…." It was a leering, teasing voice that sent shivers down my spine. "Izzy… I know you're there… I can *smell* you." Shit. It was a wolf. I looked at Izzy. Was she a wolf? It didn't matter. This man was clearly the source of her terror, and so he became the source of mine.

I could hear the man walking closer. There were some other voices in the background but I couldn't make out much. How many were there? Two? Three? Either way I was screwed, but I wasn't going down without a fight. I slowly moved my hand towards a stool that was nearby.

Izzy shook her head. I ignored her. The man stepped behind the counter to face Izzy and I made my move. I leapt up as fast as I could and swung the stool hard at the back of his head. It worked. He crumpled like a rag doll, but I wasn't quick enough. Someone else slammed into me, knocking me to the floor. I tried every defensive move I knew. Every move I had ever learned from practically growing up at the boxing gym my dad used to own. It was no use. I was pinned under the unmovable wall of muscle on top of me. I could see the man I had hit getting up. He walked over and kicked me hard in the face. I remember hearing a sickening crunch coming from my nose before passing out.

The light hurt my eyes. What little light that was reaching my eyes anyways. They were swollen and painful. I tried getting up, but immediately regretted it. I got dizzy and had to sit back down. *Slow,* I told myself. Not a word I liked based on my last conscious memory and the fact that I didn't know where I was, but better slow and quiet than fast and falling over making noise. I stood, *slowly.* It hurt. My eyes were getting used to the light and I tried to get a better look at my surroundings. I was in a small room. Well, a small cell would be more accurate. A bed, a side table, a toilet, and a sink with a small mirror above it were all that decorated the space. No windows. I shuffled my way to the door. Locked. I swore to myself. Why had I tried to fight? Why didn't I just try to make a run for it? Moving across the room had made me light-headed again, and I hurt everywhere. I chanced a glance in the small mirror. My face was a beautiful mash of colors. Blue and purple around my eyes, and dried red blood running all down my cheeks. My brown hair was a tangled mess. I lifted my shirt, apparently my face wasn't the only place those boots had kicked. The right side of my rib cage matched the colors of my face. Tears welled up in my eyes. I stopped them. I would not allow myself to cry, and I would die before being sold into slavery to any species.

There was a soft knock on the door. I turned quickly and winced from the pain. There was a figure standing in the doorway. Tall, muscular, sandy hair, and male. It was all I could make out. "Go sit." I stood my ground. "Sit. I'm here to help." I wasn't sure I believed him, but my head had started to pound and the room had started to spin. Sitting sounded good. I made my way to the edge of the bed and sat. He placed a bowl of warm water on the floor at my feet and placed a wet cloth in my hands. "I'd do it myself, but I don't know how bad you are hurting." I kept silent. "Are you hungry?" I was, but I wasn't going to give this man the satisfaction of an answer. My stomach betrayed me and growled. He shook his head and walked out, making sure to shut and lock the door on his way. I cleaned my face and walked back to the mirror. I took my hair down and tried to finger comb some of the tangles out. It was hopeless, so I put it back up in a messy bun. I heard the door opening again.

A tray of food in his hands, the man stepped back into the room. It smelled amazing. Stew with two large slices of fresh bread, and I could smell the butter! My stomach growled again. "Please come sit." He said. I didn't wait this time. I sat. "Do you have a name?" I glared at him in response. "Fine. I'm Theo. I hope you eat meat. The stew is good, it's fresh venison."

I took a small bite. It hurt to chew, but the stew was astounding. "Thank you." I hated to say it, but my mother raised me to be polite. Some habits are hard to break.

"So! She talks!"

"If you can't say anything nice"… My mother's voice popped into my head. So I kept my mouth shut but rolled my eyes. Theo laughed.

He walked towards me and bent down to retrieve the dirty water and cloth. He rung the cloth out and took another step towards me. "You missed a spot…" He paused, holding his hand slightly extended in my direction. I nodded, giving him my silent permission. He stepped closer and brushed the cloth along the side of my neck. "You're lucky Sebastian didn't kill you." So this wasn't the man who had knocked me unconscious. That made me feel a little better.

"Maybe it would have been better if he had." I whispered.

Theo stopped trying to wipe the dried blood from my neck. "No." It was all he said. He got up, grabbed the bowl of dirty water and left the tray of food for me to finish. "Get some rest." He grumbled as he walked out.

I'm not sure how long I was in there. After eating I fell back asleep and when I woke up nothing had changed, except the now empty, tray of food was gone. I needed to pee so I walked to the toilet in the far corner. After living in a camp of runaway humans, I wasn't abashed at the thought of someone walking in and seeing me pee, but I was silently grateful no one did. I washed my hands and looked in the mirror again. Some of the swelling had gone down, and without the dried blood caked on my face I looked a little better. I heard the knock again and Theo walked in. "Good, you're up. Come with me."

He stepped back outside of the room. My mind had already begun to reel with escape plans. Find an exit and run; try to knock him out and run; fight my way through who knew how many wolves and run. RUN, it was all I could think of. *This whole apocalypse/supernatural takeover sure was good for my cardio.* I laughed at the thought and realized I might still have a concussion from the beating I took…

Any thought of escape left my mind when I stepped through the door. By the look of the hallway, we were underground. I wanted to get out, but I wasn't stupid enough to think that this was the most opportune moment. Theo led me down the hall, and I tried to keep track of the several turns we made as we went. "Who taught you to fight?" he asked.

"My dad." It was all I could say without feeling my eyes begin to burn again. I missed him, and right now, I needed him. I could almost hear him say *"Keep your thoughts calm, Andie. When you forget to think, you make stupid mistakes and in a fight those mistakes will cost you."* How many times had he said those words to me when we were sparing at his gym? I focused again on trying to remember the way we traveled. From my cell we'd gone down the hall to the right, second left, first right, another twenty yards… This place was bigger than I expected. We finally came to a room with a slender, severe-looking woman standing outside of it.

"This is Trish. She will have to go into the locker room with you, but the shower stalls have doors and are private. There are some extra clothes in there for you to change into as well. I'm to escort you to meet my father when you are finished." I must have had a funny look on my face because he asked if I was OK.

"Fine. Thank you."

A shower, a real shower with hot water. It had been months. Mostly back at camp we couldn't waste the fresh water we carried for drinking in order to take a shower. When we were lucky enough to set up for the night near a creek or lake, the showers were very cold, and very short. The moment the hot water hit my skin I began to relax. I knew Trish was there, but she couldn't see me, and the shower felt so good I wouldn't have cared if she could. The hot water soothed all of my sore muscles and eased the tension in my head. Despite my bruises, I scrubbed every inch of my skin hard, until it was pink and raw. It made me feel better than I had felt in a long time. It made me feel human. Ironic, isn't it? Since I'm pretty sure the supernatural shower as well, but it made me feel human and more myself.

I stayed under the spray of water as long as I could before Trish started banging on the shower stall door and telling me to hurry up. I got out and dried off quickly. To my surprise the clothes that had been left for me were a close fit. Nothing fancy: a pair of skinny jeans and a V-neck t-shirt. But they were clean, and they didn't reek of sweat and blood like my own clothes did.

When I moved to pick up my dirty clothes, Trish told me to leave them there. I obeyed and walked out of the bathroom ahead of her. As promised, Theo was waiting to escort me. He walked over and sniffed me. It startled me and I jumped back slightly.

"What are you doing?"

"I'm smelling you."

"Why?"

He ignored the question and instead said, "Let's go see my dad."

I nodded in agreement and followed him away from the locker room.

"My father," he said as we began to walk again, "is the Alpha of our pack. Things will go better for you if you are polite, respectful, and don't stare him directly in the eye. He is generally a kind and fair man, but you are a stranger, and a human who attacked one of his pack."

"I didn't attack him. I was trying to defend myself and that girl."

He looked at me. "Izzy?"

"Yes, I think that was her name."

He shook his head before responding. "Regardless of how you see it, you would do better not to argue with my father."

We came to a stairwell and up to ground level we went. I could tell by the way the air smelled that we were no longer underground. Down another hallway, a left turn and a few more feet, and we came to a stop outside of an ornate double door. It was wood carved with one wolf on each door howling at a full moon that split down the middle and became the door handles. When Theo opened the door, I heard voices that immediately became silent. There were half a dozen people staring at me from behind a table that had been raised to sit on a platform. The rest of the room was empty of people, except for a single young man who looked extremely irritated. The rest of the room was filled with smaller tables and dozens of chairs. All of them were lower to the ground than the raised table at the front and the whole room reminded me of a large meeting room or even a courtroom. The young man I had noticed sat by himself, and I could feel his icy stare following me as I walked in.

A middle-aged man sitting at the center of the table spoke "Thank you, Theo. You may sit by Sebastian." He indicated the younger man sitting by himself. Sebastian. So this was the man I'd hit over the head with a stool, before he responded in kind by kicking the daylights out of me. *Great.*

"My name is Roderick. I am the Alpha of this pack. What is your name?" There was a very commanding tone in his voice. His hair was slightly peppered, but otherwise he looked very young. Smooth and handsome features complimented his still well-muscled form. I could tell this was a man who both deserved and was used to receiving respect.

"Andie, sir. Umm, well, Cassandra."

"Well, Cassandra. I would like to know why you and the other two humans we found were stealing from a store in my territory, and why you chose to attack my son, Sebastian." *The other two humans.* AJ and Stephen. What had happened to them? Were they here? Were they OK? Wait. Sebastian was his son? That meant Theo and he were brothers. "Cassandra. I am not accustomed to asking things twice."

"I'm sorry, sir. I was wondering about my friends."

Roderick gave me a stern look; it felt as though he were looking straight through me. "Your friends will be fine. Now please, answer my questions."

"We were in need of supplies. We lost a lot of ours when one of our tents flooded from all the rain. We weren't going to take more than we needed."

Another of the people sitting behind the table spoke up. "We? How many of you are there?"

I looked from the man who was speaking to Roderick. "I will not disclose how many are in my group. I will protect them from you at all costs, no matter the consequences for me." Roderick examined me for a moment, gave a curt nod, and motioned for me to continue. "When I heard one of my friends being attacked I hid behind the bakery counter. There was another girl there. She looked frightened. When Sebastian stepped behind the counter, I did what I could to try and protect myself and the other girl there, Izzy, is what he called her. It was not meant as an attack, but as defense, as I was in a vulnerable position." Despite Theo's warning I tried my best to stand tall and keep my chin up as I explained my side of the story.

The group of people behind the table began to whisper, but it quickly quieted down. At once, they all stood as Roderick spoke again. "Please stay where you are, Cassandra, we mean you no harm." I was nervous as they all walked towards me. It was all sort of surreal and business-like, but I did not like the fact that six full-grown werewolves were circling around me. I tried to stay as still as possible. One by one, they approached a little closer, sniffed me, and stepped back. They returned to their seats. "Sebastian, please step forward." He stood and stepped to stand right next to me. When I saw him in the store, I hadn't realized how huge he was. Broad shoulders, over six-foot-tall, and rippled muscles everywhere. Dark curly hair, cut short topped his head, but his eyes were what caught my attention. The look he gave me chilled me to the bone. It was a murderous stare, and as he stood beside me and turned to face the others a small growl escaped his lips. I noticed from the corner of my eye that Theo shifted in his chair slightly. "Sebastian, please explain to the council why you were hunting Izzy."

Sebastian growled slightly again. "Izzy," he spat the name out, "is no longer a part of our pack. She was found guilty of selling information about the pack to neighboring territories, to wolves and vampires alike. She has been captured alive and is being held until the council deems an appropriate punishment."

"Thank you, Sebastian. Now why don't you explain why, as our highest ranking officer, commander of our scouts, and our best hunter, that when standing only a few feet from this human, you did not notice that she was there?"

Sebastian clenched all the muscles in his arms, and his jaw muscles worked. He glanced at me and ground the words out. "I couldn't smell her."

Once again there were a few quick whispers exchanged between the council. "Can you smell her now?" another member asked.

"No." The word sounded like it tasted like poison in his mouth.

"Thank you, Sebastian. You are dismissed." Sebastian turned and stalked out of the room. Once the door was shut behind him, I blew some air out. I hadn't realized I had been holding my breath.

There were a few minutes of awkward silence. The council members kept looking at one another without speaking as if they could read each other's minds. Roderick addressed me again. "Cassandra, the council has discussed it and come to a conclusion. The charge of attacking Sebastian has been dropped, but you will remain here in our territory for a while longer. I assured you that your friends would be fine and they will be. They were roughed up a bit, taken to the edge of our territory, and told to leave. Nothing more. You, on the other hand, are a bit of a conundrum. As I am sure you are aware, wolves have an extremely good sense of smell. No one in this room, including Sebastian, can smell you. You don't appear to have a human scent. So you will stay here, under guard, until we know what to do with you. You will be moved to a more comfortable room, but you will not be left unguarded. Do you understand?"

They couldn't smell me? What the hell was this, some sort of weird joke? I nodded since I was too confused to speak. The council stood and filed out of a back door. Theo approached me.

"I'll show you to your new room. There are a few small cabins nearby we use for visitors sometimes." I nodded again and followed him outside. The sight that greeted me was not one I was expecting. There was a large grassy lawn outside of the building, and there were several families milling about. Some of the children were playing a game that looked similar to tag, but they were shifting as they played and it took me aback. Everyone else in the area acted as if it were the most natural thing in the world. "They are enjoying playing outside again. Wolves get a little stir crazy when we are stuck indoors for too long and with the rain..." He looked at me. "Look, I'm sorry you have to stay here, but it's for the good of the pack. You're an 'unknown' and the council can't just let you go without figuring out if you're a threat to us first."

"Your father said I didn't smell human. What does that mean?"

Theo scratched his jaw as we walked towards one of the small cabins on one side of the lawn. "It means exactly that. You don't smell human. You hardly even smell at all. Look, think of it this way: most creatures sort of have two scents. One that identifies your species, and one that is unique to only you, like a signature scent. When I catch a scent in the woods, another 'were' for example, part of the scent lets me know that whoever was there was a werewolf, and part of it is able to tell me if it's a scent I recognize, like Sebastian's, or if it's someone new. Make sense?"

"I suppose."

"Ok, now take you. To me, you sort of smell like the woods. It's very faint, but it reminds me of being outside, and I really have to focus on it to tell that it is you and not just the outside world I'm smelling. I think that's the signature part of your scent, the one specific to you. What has everyone confused is you don't have a smell that links you to one species. So I have to ask… What are you?"

We had arrived at the cabin. I opened the door, looked him in the eye, and said, "I'm human."

CHAPTER 4

What am I? The thought had crossed my mind a hundred, thousand times since Theo had asked me. I had shut the door in his face pretty hard. I hadn't meant to; so far Theo had been kind to me. Something I was sure he didn't have to do. The council meeting I had attended had been two days ago. Since then I hadn't left my small cabin. It was nice, once I took the time to look around it. It was simple and clean and had a very 'homey' feel to it. A comfortable bed, a small wood fireplace, a couch, and a kitchenette filled the main room. There was also a small bathroom with its own shower. Other than the cell I had been in when first coming here, I hadn't slept somewhere with four solid walls and a roof in almost a year. True to Roderick's word there was a guard posted outside my door twenty-four-seven. The only windows big enough for me to fit through faced the front of the cabin, so there was no use trying to sneak out of those.

Several times a day, a petite girl named Emma would come to my door to see if I needed anything. She would bring my breakfast, lunch, and dinner, and even brought me a book when I asked. She looked to be about my age, slender, with a short bob haircut and a pretty face. She didn't talk much except to ask what I needed and if I was being treated all right. I couldn't really complain. However, even without being a wolf, I was starting to feel stir-crazy being stuck inside. I made up my mind that the next time Emma came I would ask her if I was allowed outside.

The look on Emma's face told me she hadn't been expecting that question. "I'll ask," was all she answered with before handing me my lunch tray and turning around to leave. Late that afternoon there was another knock. I assumed it was Emma so I told the person outside to come in. It wasn't Emma, it was Sebastian. I froze mid-step heading to the door. "Can I help you?"

"You wanted outside. Let's go." I grabbed my hair tie (it was really the only possession I had that truly belonged to me at the moment), put my hair in a ponytail, and walked out the door. Sebastian followed only a few steps behind me. I hated it. I kept glancing backwards to make sure he wasn't going to shift, tackle me, and rip my throat out. "I won't do it," he said after maybe my fifth glance at him.

"Do what?"

"Whatever horrible thing you're thinking I'll do. At least not yet." *Great. That made me feel better.*

We walked across the big lawn that ran in front of the main house. All the moisture from the previous rains had dried up and it was a perfect spring day. My whole body began to relax a little. I had always loved spring, and moving around; being outside in the fresh air cleared my head a little. I risked a question. "How long will you keep me here?"

"As long as we need to. Go through here, please." He pointed to the beginning of a walking trail leading through a wooded area. I hesitated, but stepped through. Shortly after entering the woods, the path split.

"Where do you want me to go?"

"Anywhere. Just wander through the woods a bit. You can stay on or off the path, I wont loose you either way." I found the request odd, and I didn't miss the warning in his words, but I didn't mind either. I enjoyed the woods and was happy to be in the gentle shade of the trees surrounded by the smell of wild flowers and rich dirt.

After about twenty minutes, Sebastian instructed me that it was time to head back. Before getting too close to the cabin, I asked another question.

"Do you run? Umm, in human form I mean."

"Why?"

"I enjoy running. It's good exercise. And if I'm going to be locked up in this cabin most of the time, I'd like to get some running in, to burn off the extra energy from sitting so long." *Also to see if I could run away,* but I left that part out. He didn't answer. He didn't do anything except nod toward the cabin door, indicating for me to go in. I took one last deep breath of fresh air and went in. My dinner was sitting on the small kitchen table when I entered.

CHAPTER 5

"Andie."

"Go away Rory." I mumbled as I rolled over.

"Andie, wake up." I opened my eyes. It was still dark out. I jumped and yelped as I realized where I was and Theo's face came into better focus. I pulled the covers up to my chin. Seeing as how I didn't have any pajamas, I had simply been sleeping in my underwear.

"I brought you some shorts and a pair of sneakers. They should fit, and they'll work better than the boots you've been wearing if you want to go running with a pack of wolves." *What?* My mind was still asleep.

"Cassandra, if you want to go for a run, you have two minutes to get ready and get your butt outside." With that, he got off the edge of my bed and walked out the door. I put the clothes on quickly and headed to the door. I was still sore from the beating Sebastian had given me at the grocery store, but my bruises were now a brownish-yellow color, which told me they were healing.

Outside there were a dozen people standing around, including Sebastian and Theo. A few of them were doing some light stretches; others were talking to one another in friendly conversation. There were four other women in the group as well. I was disappointed that Emma was not one of them.

"Cassandra. You are to stay in the middle of the group. If you can't keep up, someone will leave and escort you back to your cabin." Theo informed me before he started to lead the group off. He started with a single lap around the lawn at a fast jog to warm up everyone's muscles. After that, he picked up a trail I could not see and started running full out.

The sun was starting to come up, and I could now easily see the small nature trail we were on. It was a beautiful area and the running felt good. It took everything I had to keep up with the group, but I did keep up. I never had less than three werewolves running directly around me. Clearly my thoughts of running away had been predicted. Close to an hour later we looped back to the main lawn. I was drenched in sweat and grabbing a stich in my side that had been there for the last mile. Everyone else looked as if they had just done a light workout. Some were a little short of breath, others hardly looked like it had cost them any effort at all.

"Not bad for… well, you're not human, so not bad for whatever you are." Theo joked. I turned around and my jaw practically hit the ground. My eyes had healed quite a bit in the few days since I had seen him, and wow had I been missing out! Tall, well built, and every inch of him looked like he had been chiseled from the most flawless stone on earth. The early morning light danced off of his bare chest and just a hint of sweat covered his defined six-pack abs and brow. His hair was a sandy color and had that 'just got out of bed' tousled look. Hazel eyes that I was sure in that moment could read everything about me. He was hot, damned hot, and I hadn't even noticed thanks to my previously swollen eyes and slightly blurred vision. I, on the other hand, looked like I had just been chased for over an hour, through the woods, by a pack of wolves. Which I had in fact just done, but Lord did it show on me.

He laughed. "Hello? Earth to Cassandra?"

I jerked out of my daze and apologized. "Thank you for taking me on the run," I blurted out. At which point I continued to run, straight for my cabin. No one tried to stop me. It was pretty clear where I was heading.

I walked in and made a beeline for the shower, stripping off my sweat-soaked clothes as I went. This time I opted for a cold shower. I rinsed off all the dirt and sweat, washed my hair with some of the shampoo that had been placed in there for me, and got out. I towel dried my hair, and decided to braid it. I wrapped the towel around me and stepped out of the bathroom.

"Nice legs."

Jesus! No, not Jesus. Theo. He was sitting on the edge of the bed again.

"That's twice today you have scared the crap out of me! And it's polite to knock before you enter someone's living space."

"I did knock. There was no answer so I let myself in." A sly smile crossed his lips. "I thought you might like this. Emma was going to bring it with your breakfast, but I volunteered." He handed me a pale blue cotton sundress. Dresses weren't usually my choice of clothing, but beggars can't be choosers. I took the dress and scurried back to the bathroom. When I was done changing, Theo was waiting, sitting at the table with two plates of breakfast. Bacon and cheesy omelets. I was starving after our run this morning. I sat next to Theo.

"Where do you guys get all this food?"

He looked up from eating and an expression too fleeting for me to read crossed his face. "We farm most of it. The pack owns one large farm on the other side of our territory and several smaller ones throughout our land. What we don't grow, we hunt." He looked me up and down once. "The blue looks nice on you. It brings out the color of your eyes."

"Umm. Thanks."

"You're welcome. Now eat up. We have a big day ahead of us." I didn't ask what he meant. I was too busy fighting the butterflies in my stomach while trying to eat.

Once we were finished eating, we left and started to walk across the lawn, back to the main house. "So where exactly are we?"

Theo looked at me. "What do you mean?"

"I mean where in the country? My friend Rory and I grew up in Chicago. When we decided to leave, we headed west. That was a long time ago. I don't know which part of the country I'm in now."

"Oh," he said. "We are in Wyoming. Just South of the Montana boarder. Or what used to be, anyways."

Wyoming. A long way from what used to be home. I hoped Rory was doing OK without me. We had come so far together, protecting each other, learning to survive together. I missed him. I had no idea where he and the rest of my group might be by now, or how I would find them once the pack let me go.

"You all right? You look kind of sad."

"I'm fine. I was just thinking about someone. That's all."

"Someone special?"

"Yes. His name is Rory. I've known him since we were kids."

"Is he your boyfriend?"

"What? No! I mean, we tried once, but it was too weird for me. He's like my brother." I'm not sure why I felt so defensive when he asked that question. It felt like I needed to make it very clear to him that Rory and I were just friends. Not that it would matter to him, Theo was way out of my league. Girls like me didn't date guys that looked like they were descended from the Greek Gods themselves. *And it shouldn't matter to me either. He's a werewolf. End of story.* I coughed in an attempt to try and clear both my head and my suddenly dry throat. "So…" I stuttered. "What is it that we're doing?"

"We're going to meet with my father again." I paled at his words. "Not the whole council, just my father. I'll be there too." This didn't help to calm my nerves. I think I would rather have the whole council again than be locked in a room with just Roderick and Theo.

When we entered the room with the carved door there was no one inside. Theo kept walking and led me through another door behind the council table. Theo opened the door, and I stepped into a large and comfortable office. It smelled like wood polish, but there was an open window and a nice breeze was blowing across the room. Roderick was sitting behind the only desk in the room.

"Please sit." Roderick motioned to the two chairs sitting on the opposite side of his desk. Theo and I both sat. The chairs were made of comfortable brown leather with plenty of cushioning. "Cassandra, you and I have some things that need to be discussed. As my Beta, or my second-in-command, Theo will be here while I conduct this interview as well." His Beta? I had no idea. I knew Theo was his son, and I knew he must have been high up in the ranks, but his Beta? Suddenly the butterflies in my stomach got worse. I shouldn't have eaten so much after such a long run.

"Let's start with YOU, shall we? Just the basics, where you are from, your family, etc." I stared at him for a moment, took a breath, and began to talk. I knew that the more cooperative I was the easier things would go for me. So far my captors had treated me more than fairly. So much so that I'm not sure I could honestly say our group would have treated a prisoner with such respect, if we ever did happen to capture a wolf or a vamp and manage to contain them.

"I grew up in Chicago near the city. Both my parents are dead. I was an only child. They weren't able to conceive on their own, so they adopted me as a baby. When they died, I tried to find my birth parents, but there were no records of who they were or where I came from. I have been on the run for the past four years, moving from place to place with my friend Rory."

"Was he one of the young men at the store with you?"

"No, Rory wasn't there."

"So you have no idea who your birth parents are?"

"No, but it doesn't matter. My parents are dead. They were the ones who raised me."

"It does matter, Cassandra, if we are going to figure out just what it is you are."

"I'm human. Why do I have to keep saying that?!" *And why was I arguing with the Alpha of a werewolf pack?* Immediately the atmosphere in the room changed. I could feel it with every part of my body.

"You will not raise your voice to me, Cassandra." His tone was cold, and full of power. I tried to look him in the eye but couldn't. My head bowed slightly and I squeaked out an apology. The tension in the room eased a bit. "I know this must be hard to hear, Cassandra, but you are not human." His tone was a bit softer, more sympathetic.

My eyes started to burn, but I would not cry in front of these two men. I wouldn't let it happen. I sniffed. "Why does it matter what I am? Why can't I just go home?" Wherever home might be these days.

I missed my real home so much it hurt. I missed the tiny apartment I shared with my parents. I missed my room, with all of its familiar clutter. I missed the nights I would stay late with my dad at the gym he owned. We would come home and my mother would scold him for keeping me out so late, but it always ended with him kissing her gently as she sighed and heated up the diner she had made for us. I would never have those things back. The home I had on the road was temporary. The group Rory and I had run into was heading for Oregon. Andre had said he heard rumors that there was an all-human town hidden in the mountains there. Figuring Oregon sounded as good a place as any, we had joined up, doing our best to fit in with the group of strangers that had clumped themselves together to try and stay alive.

Roderick's sigh brought me back to reality. "I'm sorry Cassandra, I cannot let you leave until I know for sure whether or not you could be a danger to this pack. This pack is my family, and I will protect every single person in it with every bit of power I have until I die." I nodded, understanding how he felt. "How old are you, Cassandra?"

"I'm nineteen. I'll be twenty May third."

"That's next week." It was the first time Theo had spoken since we entered the room. I didn't know it was that close to my birthday. It made me a bit sad to think that I would no longer be a teenager, and even sadder to know that I might not get to celebrate the fact with Rory.

"I think that is enough for today," said Roderick. "Theo, why don't you show her around?"

Theo gave me the grand tour of the main house. Besides Roderick's office and the council meeting room, there were about a dozen bedrooms, half a dozen bathrooms, a large kitchen that looked like it had been updated in the past few years, a dining room that sat roughly twenty, and an entertainment room, complete with large screen TV, pool table, books, and board games. The basement, Theo explained, was used mostly for storage now. But it used to be a sort of safe haven. It had been used for 'were' families that were on the run before the world learned of their existence and needed a place to hide, for new wolves that had been bitten and changed while they learned to control their inner wolves, and occasionally when the pack had large gatherings and needed extra rooms for people to stay. The cell I had been in was one of two that were used to hold people captive. The girl Izzy was still being held in the other one. Apparently it was very rare that they needed to 'arrest' one of their own, so the cells had hardly ever been used.

"The property of the pack is quite extensive. We were lucky. Our territory includes the three small farms and one large farm I mentioned earlier, a large river, plenty of wooded areas and hills, and over thirty separate houses that the different families of the pack live in."

As we continued to walk around, I decided to ask Theo something I had been curious about for a very long time. "Why did you decide to let the world know you existed?" I couldn't look at him when I asked. I couldn't look at him at all without catching myself staring at every feature he had: his strong jaw and straight nose, his deep set, pensive eyes that burned right through me, his blondish-brown hair that was the perfect length to run your fingers through…. *crap*. Now I *was* staring at him. I blushed, half out of embarrassment and half out of frustration with myself for thinking about such things and changed the direction of my stare to the scenery ahead of me.

He grinned and then answered my question. "For centuries, werewolves, vampires, and witches had been hunted and killed by humans. Each of our three races were in danger of becoming extinct. So we went into hiding. We kept to ourselves as best we could, and slowly, over the decades our numbers began to grow again. When the 2000s came around and vampire and werewolf books and movies became the next big thing, we had hope that we might be able to reveal ourselves to the world again. To stop worrying constantly about hiding who and what we are – it was a hope all three races had. For almost a decade, we planned and prepared. The time it took to do all the planning is what allowed our pack to be so well set up. Roderick started right away buying more land for our territory and making sure that the farms were operating well. He wanted us to be self-sufficient before we came out to the public.

All three races were in on the reveal. It was a big deal. Most of the time our races don't get along very well. Werewolves have always leaned more towards protecting humans, vampires hunt them, and witches for the most part are a 'neutral' entity. They answer to nature, to the balance of good and evil. Vampires and werewolves have always been enemies, so the fact that we were able to collaborate on such an event was unprecedented. I don't think any of us expected for the humans to become the race now on the brink of extinction. While we were hoping for acceptance, we were also expecting more of a resistance from at least some of the human population.

We weren't expecting so many of you to want to join us. A lot of the werewolf packs are actually pretty upset about it. The vampires were thrilled at first. All the Donors they could ever want, ready and willing. But since their food supply is now running low, they are beginning to panic."

I hadn't expected such an explanation. I was grateful for it, to have a little more understanding, but part of what he said didn't make sense to me. "Why are the wolves so upset about losing the humans?" Everything I knew about werewolves had led me to believe that most of them were rather indifferent to whether humans survived or not.

"Werewolves never hunted humans. We are pack animals, and our instinct is to protect those lower in rank within the pack. Since humans are a weaker species, less dominant, it spurs our inner wolf to become protective of them. We only really ever harmed humans if they were threatening a pack in some way or another. I'm not saying there aren't some bad apples, so to speak. Like Izzy. When she found it would benefit her, her loyalty to the pack swayed, and she was willing to sell information about us to our enemies. For the most part though, we like to keep things peaceful when we can."

I was amazed he had opened up so much to me. It touched me, to have him trust me with this information, considering he knew me so little. I suppose none of it would be considered any great secret anymore, but it still made me happy.

"I think we had better head back. It's getting late, neither of us have had lunch, and it's nearly dinner time. I'll take you back to your cabin." We walked in silence the rest of the way, but it was a comfortable silence.

The next five days passed in routine. Emma kept me fed and brought me a new book to read. Every other morning I would go for a run with the pack. I learned that the run was something Theo led every other day. It was required of no one, but open to anyone in the pack wishing to join that day. Theo had admitted that they normally ran in wolf form, but since I had joined, he had kept everyone in human form so that I could keep up. No one seemed to be bothered by it. Most of them enjoyed running in either their human or their wolf form.

Running quickly became my favorite part of the day. Not just for the exercise, but I began to notice that I would push myself more and more so I could run closer to Theo. He ran without a shirt, and watching his back and shoulder muscles move as he ran made my mouth dry. His running shorts always hung low on his hips and running behind him gave me an excellent view of his strong legs and firm butt. Theo and a few of the others began to take note of how well I ran. Apparently, it was not expected of me to be able to keep pace with a bunch of werewolves, even in their human form.

The sixth morning after my first run, I woke up early on my own, knowing that we would be running today. I now had three changes of clothes that were being rotated and washed for me, I assumed by Emma. I got dressed and waited. No one came to get me. I began to wonder if I had simply mixed up the days, but no. Theo had told me that they organized a run every other morning no matter rain or shine. I looked out the window. My guard was there as always, but rather than watching my door, he was looking in the opposite direction. I opened the window and shouted to him. He turned and quickly told me to shut up and be quiet. I did so, but I left the window open and went to sit quietly and listen. Something was happening and I wanted to know what it was. I heard some howling in the distance and my stomach sank. It was not the kind of playful howl I'd heard several times since coming here, but a short, eerie howl. It was followed by several other howls and a single wolf yelping in pain. I ran back to the window. It looked as if my guard had run off at first, but then my line of sight dropped a little lower. There was a large brown wolf standing in front of my cabin now. His hackles were raised and he was snarling in the direction the noise was coming from. Aside from the growling coming from my guard, all was silent. It took a long time for anyone to appear. When they did, it didn't feel like good news. The biggest wolf I had ever seen came sprinting towards the cabin. It was all black, and moved at a speed I didn't know was possible. He came to a halt in front of my guard. They stood there for a moment merely looking at each other before my guard dipped his head to the black wolf and ran off. The other wolf bounded up to the porch in two quick steps. As it landed in front of the door it shifted. A very angry looking Sebastian stood where the wolf had been and I jumped backwards just as he ripped open the door.

"You! Come with me!" He grabbed my arm and shoved me out the door. I stumbled, but he pushed me again to keep me moving.

"What happened?" I asked. His response was a deep snarl that came from his chest. He took me to the main house and led me to the council room.

When the door opened I gasped. It looked as if there were fifty people in the room. All of them fell silent when I walked in. Theo was standing near the council table. The look on his face made me sick. He couldn't hide the anger he was feeling. Though it didn't feel as if it were directed at me, I couldn't even look at him. Worse was the look Roderick gave me. The hatred and disgust in the look he gave me made me shiver. I had no idea what had happened, but all signs pointed to it being my fault.

Sebastian shoved me roughly into a chair in the middle of the room and stood behind me. I felt tiny, both physically and emotionally, compared to the men and women in this room.

Roderick spoke as if he had no doubt I had known all along exactly what had happened. "Cassandra. If you are not aware, this morning there was a small group of humans that invaded our territory. One of my pack was injured, and one of the humans was killed."

I was going to vomit. Oh no. No, no, no, no!

"Before he died, the boy spoke your name. Apparently, they were on some kind of fool mission to rescue you. Why would a small group of humans take such a risk, knowing they would be outnumbered and unable to match the strength we present!?" Roderick terrified me.

"I don't know!" I said. I tried desperately to make him believe me. "Please, I don't know! They should have moved on by now. If I didn't come back to camp, they should have left without me!"

But I already knew whom it was that had stayed behind. Who would have risked anything to save me. My heart sank.

"Stop lying! Perhaps the human boy risked so much because he knew your secret. Tell me what you are!" The power and force in his voice rumbled throughout the room. Even Theo shrank back from his father a bit. I felt like I was being crushed and suffocated by his voice. I wanted so desperately to be anywhere but here.

"I don't know…" I whimpered.

"Louder!" Roderick yelled.

Something in me snapped. Alpha or no, what had happened was not my fault and it was time to yell back. "I don't know!" I was not the only one there taken by surprise at the power and strength of my own voice. Even Roderick gave me a quizzical look. This time I stared him straight in the eyes. "I don't know what I am. All my life I have believed without a doubt that I am a human. And other than my scent you have no evidence to support that I'm not one. The people I traveled with should not have come for me. They had to have known it would be too great of a risk, especially with no proof that I was still alive. You can yell at me all you like, but I had nothing to do with this." Roderick's face had turned a dark reddish-purple as I spoke and a large vein throbbed across his forehead.

"We will see about that. Bring the boy in," he barked. The door behind me opened and I could hear someone walking in. I turned and the room around me seemed to disappear. There was someone walking down the middle of the room carrying a limp body. The size of the body, the color of his skin, the AC/DC shirt I had given him for his birthday years ago that he still wore, and his frazzled-looking dark brown hair... I recognized it all. I stood but after one step towards him I fell to my knees. The man carrying him laid him on the ground unceremoniously in front of me. Rory. Sweet, clumsy Rory. He must have convinced the others to come back for me. He was the only family I had left in this world, and now he was gone. I did not try to stop the tears this time. I let them fall without shame. He was my brother, my best friend, and they had killed him.

My blood was boiling I was so enraged, and it felt as though my heart had been ripped out of my chest.

"Enough," said Roderick. "Take her back to the basement cell." And back to the tiny room I had first woken up in I went, my back straight and crying silently the whole way.

They left me alone. They did not bring me any food. There were no friendly knocks on the door. I didn't care. I cried all day and must have eventually cried myself to sleep. I woke to the sound of someone coming into the room. I kept my eyes closed. I didn't want to talk.

"Cassandra..." His voice was soft. "Cassandra, I am so sorry..." It was all Theo said. I could tell he stood in the doorway for another minute, either trying to think of something else to say or waiting for me to respond before he walked back out.

The next morning when they came to get me, I had no more tears to shed. I knew I looked like hell, but it didn't matter. They could do whatever they wanted to me now. Sebastian didn't have to speak when he opened the door. I stood automatically and walked out into the hall with him. I remembered the way to the council room, and I let myself in. Sebastian followed silently. Roderick, the rest of the council members, and Theo were waiting for me. There was also a woman I did not recognize. Her long silver hair was in a plaited braid that reached her waist. She was slender, but well-muscled and she had friendly laugh lines around her bright green eyes. Despite her apparent age, she was beautiful.

"Hello, Cassandra." Her voice had a musical aspect to it. Regardless of the gaping hole in my chest where my heart used to be, I was drawn to this woman. I trusted her immediately. "Come here." I walked towards her. "I need a table." She stated to no one in particular. Theo pulled a small one from the side of the room and pushed it in between us. She reached into a large bag she had with her and pulled out a small glass bowl and a small golden dagger. She laid them next to each other on the table. She also pulled from her bag four candles, which she placed around the bowl. She then looked to Roderick. "Alpha, do I have your permission to do magic in this house?" Roderick stood in front of the dais where the council usually sat, his chest puffed out, his arms crossed, and gave a terse nod.

"My name is Anthea. Please, hold out your hand above the bowl." As she spoke the candles lit of their own accord. I did as she asked. She placed my hand on top of hers, palms facing up, and picked the dagger up in her other hand. "In order to perform the species identifying spell, I will need some of your blood. It will only hurt a little." She slid the dagger down my palm, which stung, but only for a moment. Once a small pool of blood had formed in my hand she tipped it so that the blood dripped into the bowl. She let go of my hand and I stepped back from the table. Anthea grabbed some type of herb from the belt that was wrapped around her skirt. Speaking some words I could not understand, she used one of the candles to light the herb on fire and then placed it in the bowl. She continued to speak the unfamiliar words and a cloud of smoke formed above the bowl. Anthea stopped talking and waited. I followed her gaze to the cloud of smoke, which all of a sudden began to change color and shape repeatedly. With each change, the expression on Anthea's face changed as well;

from intrigue, to confusion, to disbelief. The cloud of smoke disappeared and Anthea's eyes snapped up to meet mine. "surAvani." She whispered the word as if it were a secret. When she said it, I felt a jolt of heat run down my spine. Anthea stepped around the table, bent to her knees, and placed her forehead on the floor at my feet. She began to speak in the strange language again, almost as if saying a prayer.

Everyone seemed to be at a loss as Anthea continued to pray at my feet. Theo stepped forward and pressed a rag into my injured hand; it was still bleeding and had begun to drip on the floor. "What's happening?" I asked him.

"I'm not sure," he whispered back.

After several minutes Anthea rose, tears of joy streaming down her face. "surAvani. I am honored." She took my uninjured hand, kissed the back of it, and bent down to press her forehead to the skin her lips had just left.

"Well?!" Roderick demanded. "What is she?"

Anthea turned to face him. "She is a blessing to us all. A gift. She is the surAvani." When no one appeared to know what that meant, Anthea asked as politely as she could for everyone to sit. They did so reluctantly. Apparently werewolves weren't so comfortable taking orders from a witch. Theo stayed standing by my side in the middle of the room.

"Cassandra is in fact not human."

CHAPTER 6

It felt as though I had taken a blow to the chest. I was so confused. Who and what was I then? Anthea approached me deliberately, and gently placed my face in her hands. Her eyes beamed with pride. "I never thought that in my lifetime I would get to meet you. And I have lived a very long time." She addressed the room again. "As you all know, witches serve the balance of good and evil. We draw our strength and wisdom from nature. We have a legend..."

"No damn legend, just tell me what the child is!" Roderick stated. He was clearly losing his patience with Anthea.

"May I remind you Alpha, that you asked me to come here and I did so willingly to help? Now please, let me explain everything at once." Roderick did not respond and so Anthea continued. "We witches have a legend. Long ago when the world was still full of all manner of magical creatures, the earth was ruled by nature, by the Goddess, the All Mother... you know her as Mother Earth. We witches knew her as surAvani. When humans were born, and they began to consume the world and take it as their own, the All Mother lost many of her own children. As she lost her children, she also began to lose her powers. So she made a decision. Once every millennium, she would bear a child, one of her own blood, in hopes that this child would be able to do what she could not, and return the balance of all species to the world. The child would be a female. And she would be a Nymph, the most powerful one of all. That is what Cassandra is. She is the daughter of Mother Earth, her species is that of the nymphs from the old world. She carries the blood of the All Mother in her veins. And she is the greatest gift we could ever have hoped for." She turned to face me again. Her eyes were still shining with tears. She bowed her head and said, "surA-vani, I am at your service. My spirit and my powers are yours to command."

I was in shock. So was everyone else.

"But… the Nymphs… they've been extinct for centuries…"

"How is this possible?"

"The daughter of Mother Earth?"

The whispers were quiet at first, but then they started to grow louder. I noticed that at some point during Anthea's explanation I had grabbed Theo's hand. He was holding it tightly and the realization surprised me. "Cassandra, are you all right?" he asked. I hardly knew how to answer. I felt so strange, and still so confused.

"If she is who you say she is," Roderick asked, "then why is it she has no special powers?"

"She does." Anthea answered him. "But they must be released. It takes a ritual, done outside in nature, to release the bonds she has to the human world and to open up her spirit to her true self." She grabbed my hand excitedly. "We could do it tonight! The ritual requires a full moon and there is one tonight!" This woman I had barely just met was so happy. The excitement and joy that emanated from her touched me.

I looked at Theo with the question in my eyes. He looked concerned and he was still holding on to me. With his free hand he gently tucked a piece of hair behind my ear and so nobody but me could hear said, "It's your choice, Andie." To hear my old nickname come from his lips made some-thing warm curl deep in my belly. I was terrified of what it would mean, but I looked at Roderick, and then to Anthea and nodded my agreement.

While Anthea was thrilled, Roderick appeared less so. Anthea was already spouting out thoughts of her entire coven coming to help with the ritual, and about taking me to live with them. At the mention of me leaving I thought I heard a small growl come from Theo's chest. However, Roderick stopped Anthea right there and they began to argue about what would happen to me. While everyone was distracted with the two of them,

Theo pulled me across the room where it was less crowded. "Are you sure about this?" he asked.

"I'm not sure about anything anymore. Yesterday, I was still a human, Rory was alive, and I knew my place in the world. But if this is what I am then I might as well learn all I can about it. If there's one thing I've learned in my lifetime, it's that when things change, you had better learn to accept it, and fast."

Theo tipped my chin up with his knuckle and looked me in the eyes. It made my stomach do that weird warm curling again, and my heart beat a little faster. "I knew you had to be special." He leaned in close to me then, the smell of him was intoxicating; musk mixed with spice, it made me dizzy and weak in the knees to have him pressed this close to me. It was a feeling I was unsure I wanted. "Happy birthday, Cassandra." He whispered it in my ear, pressed a gentle kiss to my cheek, and then he left. By the time I regained my senses, he had already left the council room. It was my birthday.

CHAPTER 7

RODERICK AND ANTHEA FINALLY CAME TO AN AGREEMENT OF sorts. Neither party was very happy, but I suppose that is part of negotiating. Roderick said he would allow two additional witches onto the property to help Anthea with the ceremony. They would be allowed to take me into the woods unguarded, but they were to return me to the pack once the ceremony was over. The last part had been non-negotiable. While I had agreed to the ceremony, the fact that I had no say in the rest of what was to happen left a bitter taste in my mouth.

Not long after, the other two witches Anthea had asked to join us showed up. The three of them together were somewhat comical. Although I learned that they were all well over five hundred years old, they all looked to be anywhere from their late forties to early sixties, but with the news of what I was they were all three acting like schoolgirls giggling at a sleepover. Roderick allowed us the use of one of the bigger rooms on the main floor of the house to prepare. The other two witches introduced themselves as Dorothy and Florence. Florence was the head witch of their coven and before embracing me warmly, they both greeted me in a similar fashion to what Anthea had done when she kissed my hand and then bent to press her forehead to the same spot. We all went into the bedroom together and they sent me to the private attached bathroom to bathe. Once I was in the tub the three of them came in. I was slightly embarrassed, but the other women had no concerns about seeing my naked body and so I began to relax. They washed my hair with an aloe-smelling cream, and gave me a lovely lavender scented soap to scrub with. When I was finished, and wrapped in a towel, Anthea sat with me, towel drying my hair and brushing it until it shined and looked the color of melted chocolate. She added some delicate braids throughout and stuck an assortment of flowers in. Florence asked me to stand and remove the towel. I did as she asked. I again felt awkward at first but once I realized that they didn't care I was naked, I stopped caring as well. Florence then started to rub a silver powder all over my body. I was plenty pale on my own, but the powder made my skin take on the appearance of moonlight. Dorothy came over carrying a dress. "Dress" was a loose term, in my opinion. It was white in color and practically sheer. It was full length, its hem just brushing the tops of my feet. It also had two large slits, one on each side causing my legs to show up to my thighs when I walked. The deep V-neck front plunged between my breasts and showed a hint of cleavage. I wasn't well endowed in that department, but the dress helped to accentuate what little curves I had. Lastly, Anthea smudged a little red coloring onto my lips. When I was done being dressed the three of them stepped back, all beaming.

I turned to look at myself in the mirror and was pleasantly surprised. Where I expected to see plain old me, I saw a young woman. My skin was glowing, my dark rich hair was exquisitely pinned up and my blue eyes looked brighter than ever before. My eyes fell to rest on my red lips, which looked lush and full. I stood staring at myself in disbelief for a few minutes before the three women told me it was time to leave.

I followed them back out into the hallway that would lead past the council room and out the front door. Theo was standing outside the open carved doors of the council room, talking to one of the pack members. He fell silent the moment he saw me. The burning stare he sent me brought color to my cheeks and my stomach felt like it had flip-flopped. He didn't say anything, but continued to stare as I walked past him and out onto the open lawn. It was already getting dark out, and a large portion of the pack was gathered on the far side of the lawn.

The witches led me out into the woods heading away from the group that had gathered. Anthea grabbed my hand as we walked. "We are headed towards the river that cuts through this territory. It will provide the best location for the ceremony."

"I'm nervous."

"As you should be." She paused before speaking again. "There is something you should know, Cassandra. I am not entirely sure what will happen once we break your bond with the human world. I imagine that a great amount of power will flood your body. Not even I can predict how your body will respond to it. It will be quite a shock to your system, and it will take some time getting used to, and even more time to learn to control that power."

I took a deep breath to calm my nerves and nodded. After all, what did I have left to lose if things went badly?

It was quite a walk from the main house to the river. I was barefoot, but the moss-covered path we followed was quite soft and didn't hurt to walk on.

We finally arrived at the river. There was a small clearing next to it and Florence politely asked me to sit and wait while they got a few things ready for the ceremony. I walked to a large log and sat to wait. Every nerve was on end, and I was starting to feel a little sick to my stomach. The rational part of my brain began to protest what I was about to commit to so I tried to focus solely on the three women as they built a large bonfire and lit it with magic. They also set a large number of candles out across the clearing, each one lighting on its own as the witches placed them on the ground. I could tell it was almost time. Anthea had told me the ceremony would take place when the full moon was at its highest peak. Did I really want this? Was I ready for it? My mind began to protest again.

A dark blur bolted from the woods and came to a halt by my side. "Oh no! No wolves allowed!" Dorothy admonished the animal.

The wolf whined and pranced his front paws. It cocked its head sideways to look at me. I gasped. "Theo?" The wolf sat down and bobbed his head in what I assumed was a nod yes. His eyes were the same burning hazel that felt like they pierced straight through me. "Can he stay? Please. I would like him here with me." As unsure about my feelings for Theo as I was, his presence helped to calm me.

The witches didn't look too happy but they didn't argue, they simply told him to make sure when the time came he stayed out of the way. I got down on my knees next to Theo. His fur was a deep russet color, one minute red, the next it looked brown. It complemented the color of his eyes. He was large, but sleek. I could tell he would be quick as lightning in his wolf form. I reached my hand out and stroked his fur. He shuddered slightly but didn't do anything that told me I should stop. His fur was soft, but the muscle underneath was hard as stone. I reached again, this time to scratch him behind the ear. He groaned in pleasure. "Thank you for coming," I whispered. He licked my hand and turned his watchful attention to the witches.

"It's time," Florence said. I stood and so did Theo. Florence shot him a look and he stayed put, but remained on all four paws. I walked towards the fire. "Cassandra, please take a handful of earth in one hand." I followed Florence's instructions and reached down to grab some of the soft river sand. From there, Dorothy handed me a branch she had been holding over the fire. It was long enough that I was in no danger of being burned, but the other end was blazing. "Now please, surAvani, step into the river. You need only to be ankle deep." I looked at Theo again. His steady gaze gave me courage and I stepped into the river. I turned to face the three witches who had formed a line facing me and were holding each other's hands. As soon as they began to speak, the water around my ankles started to bubble, and a steady wind picked up.

"Mighty All Mother, hear us now. Your daughter is here surrounded by the five elements: Water, Earth, Fire, Air, and Spirit. She has come to claim her right, to follow in your footsteps, to right the balance of good and evil in the world. Bless her, oh Mother, for she is yours." They started to chant in unison, in the strange language I had heard Anthea use before. The wind picked up even more, whipping my hair around my face. The fire on the branch I was holding was burning brighter, a small plant had started to sprout out of the earth I was holding in my other hand, and the water bubbled up to my knees, soaking my dress. It suddenly felt like my body was being consumed by both fire and ice at once. I could no longer hear what the witches were saying. I couldn't see anything except a blinding white light. I don't know how long it lasted. It could have been a year, or it could have been the briefest of moments. And then it was over, and there was only darkness.

CHAPTER 8

I HEARD SPLASHING AND A MAN'S VOICE YELLING. I WAS WET.
The water was cold, but the temperature of it seemed to have no effect on
me now. I felt strong arms picking me up before things went dark again.
The next flash of consciousness I had was of being carried through the
woods. Bright images of plants and the smell of rich soil permeated my
senses. I could hear someone panting. I passed out again.

The first thing I noticed when I woke up was a tingling sensation.
Not the kind you feel when your arm falls asleep, more like my whole body
was alive with energy. My body felt like it was humming. I opened my eyes
and it took a moment for my sight to adjust. It was like seeing the world
in high definition. Colors were brighter; every shape was more defined
and more intriguing, and a million different smells assaulted my nostrils. I
could hear the soft breathing of someone else in the room so I turned my
head just an inch to look at my surroundings. I was in the bedroom I had
gotten ready in with Anthea and the other witches. I was lying on a very
comfortable bed with the covers pulled up to my shoulder. Only my arms
and head were exposed. I looked for the source of the breathing and found
it quickly. Sitting in a chair placed near the foot of the bed was Theo. He
had fallen asleep and was bent forward with his head resting by my feet.
His arm was outstretched, his fingers only an inch away from mine.

I tried to move and groaned. Holy cow was I sore! The noise woke Theo. He jumped up and looked around the room before his gaze turned to me. "Andie." He breathed my name like a sigh of relief.

"Hey there," I managed to croak out.

"Andie, don't try to move. I'll be right back with Anthea." He dashed out the door. Having never been very good at following orders. I painfully managed to work my way into a sitting position before Theo and Anthea walked back in the door. "Do you ever listen to what you're told?" Theo asked. He walked around the side of the bed and scooted the chair he had been in before closer to my head before regaining his seat.

"Here, drink this." Anthea handed me a coffee mug filled with a hot liquid. "It's an herbal tea. It will help you feel better."

I took a sip and shot Theo a look that said *See? I can follow instructions.* He smiled and shook his head. "How long have I been out?" As soon as the question left my lips, Theo's expression fell, but it was Anthea who answered my question.

"There is much to discuss, Cassandra. Theo, I will fetch your father and we can all discuss it together." Theo nodded and Anthea walked out of the bedroom.

Grabbing my hand, Theo said, "Tell me you're all right."

"I'm fine. Really. I feel a bit strange, but in a good way. Very sore though." The tea was helping to make me feel more alert and was soothing my dry throat, making it easier to talk.

"How long was I out?" I asked again.

"Three days."

He seemed exhausted. Light shadows under his eyes were the only thing that marred his still beautiful features. Three days... what had happened in that time? I must have looked as though I were about to speak because Theo beat me to it. "Just rest for a moment. We'll discuss everything with you as soon as Roderick gets here."

To keep him happy I sat quietly and sipped my tea. A light blush crept across my cheeks as Theo continued to stare at me. "Stop staring. I'm not running away any time soon."

"I hope you never run away."

The whispered words startled me. He didn't want me to leave? I didn't have time to analyze his statement any further because Roderick and Anthea came back through the door just then. "I am glad to see you are awake, Cassandra." Roderick said, and he sounded as though he truly meant it. They both found chairs and sat; Roderick and Anthea on one side of the bed, Theo on the other.

"Now will you tell me what happened?." It was hard to keep the whine from my voice.

Roderick cleared his throat. "First and foremost, Cassandra, I believe I owe you an apology. I was unnecessarily harsh with you the day your friends attacked us. I've learned that the young man who died was very close to you, and I am sorry for your loss."

The thought of Rory made tears come to my eyes. Stiff as Roderick's apology was, I did not think he was a man who apologized often and so it meant a great deal that he apologized at all. "Thank you." I responded quietly.

He nodded slightly and spoke again. "There is something else I must apologize for as well. Izzy, the young wolf you first saw in the grocery store, was being held in the basement in the cell next to yours. She was being held until the council had time to discuss whether her crime of selling information about our pack was worthy of execution or not."

Execution? My eyes widened at the word.

"I know that sounds like a harsh punishment, but betrayal is not something we take lightly in this pack, nor is the punishment of execution, which is why a decision has not yet been made. While I am Alpha and the decision is ultimately mine, the council is made up of some older, and very wise, werewolves and I value their opinions highly, but I digress. Izzy was still in her cell the night of the full moon. We were unaware until now that there is an air vent that leads from the council room to her cell. She was able to hear everything Anthea said about what you are."

A feeling of dread started to form in my stomach like a sinking rock. Izzy had been captured because she was selling information about the pack to their enemies.

"On nights of the full moon, all members of the pack are invited to run as a group through the grounds. It is by no means mandatory, but quite a few of our members join in. There were only two guards left at the main house, and Izzy was able to escape. She killed one of the guards on her way out. We can only assume she was the one who sold the information about you to the vampires." The stone in my stomach plummeted. "The vampire coven that has a territory just west of us attacked last night. They were attempting to come and kill you, Cassandra. Since Izzy was still my responsibility, it is only right that I accept responsibility for your life being threatened."

"The vampires tried to kill me? Why?"

"We aren't entirely sure." It was Anthea who answered. "My coven and I are trying to find all the information we can about what you are and what you will be able to do, but there isn't much. The best we can figure is that with your new power you either pose a threat to their way of life somehow, or perhaps they sought to kidnap you and use your powers to their benefit."

"I will not let them hurt you." I looked at Theo. Determination and conviction shone on his face. I wanted to hug him. Instead, we sat staring at each other in silence until Roderick cleared his throat again.

"There were only a few of them that formed the attack. We were lucky; we had several injured but no deaths on our end, and we heal quickly. We were able to kill two of the vampires that attacked, but the rest retreated back to their own land. I have a feeling that next time, we will not be so lucky."

Roderick's words haunted me. "What are we going to do?"

"Right now, I think it is best that you get some rest. I have agreed to allow Anthea to remain on the property for now. She is staying in the room next to yours."

Anthea stood, stating that rest sounded good and excused herself by bowing slightly and whispering the name surAvani. Roderick inclined his head ever so slightly toward me and chose to follow Anthea out.

CHAPTER 9

THEO REMAINED SITTING WHERE HE WAS. HE RUBBED HIS hands over his face and sighed.

"Did you stay in here all night?" I asked Theo quietly.

The tired look on Theo's face tugged lightly at my heart.

"Would you be mad if I said yes?"

"No. I would be mad if you lied."

He looked deep into my eyes. "I have not left this room since the moment I picked you up out of the creek and carried you here."

I sucked in a deep breath of air. "What about when the vampires attacked?"

"I was here, standing guard over you while you slept. One of the vampires made it in here. She was one of the two who died." I looked around the room, expecting to see a pool of blood somewhere. Theo followed my gaze. "They don't bleed. Listen to me carefully, Cassandra, because there may come a time when you need to know this. There are only a few ways to kill a vampire. Stake them in the heart with wood, burn them with sunlight or decapitate them. When they die, they simply turn into a pile of ash." I didn't want to ask how this vampire died, but I suspected I knew the answer. "Get some rest." He started to stand up.

"Wait..."

He waited.

"Will you stay tonight too?" It made me nervous to say it, but I did want him to stay. I felt safer with him here.

"Do you want me to?"

I gave a very small nod.

His face broke into a wide grin. "Scoot over." I was frozen. What did he mean? "I've spent the last three nights sleeping in that chair. If you want me to stay, scoot over. I'll behave. Promise." That sly grin was on his face again. I tried to channel my mother and gave him the best *You had better behave* look I could muster. He laughed loudly and climbed onto the bed. He stretched out and sighed in contentment as he tucked his hands under the back of his head.

"Make yourself comfortable." There may have been some sarcasm in my voice.

"I had planned on it." He winked.

His face became more serious as he told me to lie down. "I'll stay above the covers."

I gave in, lying on my side so we faced each other. "You saved my life. Thank you."

"No need to thank me. I will always protect you."

"Is that because you see me as a weaker person you need to protect?"

His brow furrowed. "I don't think there is a single weak bone in your body, Cassandra."

I scoffed. "I doubt that…"

He rolled over so he was on his side, his head propped up by one hand. "I'm not kidding. From the moment I met you, you have been incredibly strong. Maybe not physically…" he teased, "but, you didn't hesitate when you hit Sebastian at the store, even though you didn't know who your enemy was. You fought back, hard, when I tackled you afterwards, and you have stood up to an Alpha werewolf while staring him directly in the eye. No Cassandra, I do not think you are weak."

I didn't know what to say. I had a drop-dead gorgeous man lying next to me in bed, telling me how strong I was, and my mind was blank! "I didn't know you were the one who tackled me." *Smooth, Cassandra… smooth.*

The corners of his mouth twitched up. "I'd like to tackle you again."
Oh my! The thought of Theo tackling me, the weight of his body pressed on top of me... I blushed again.

Theo reached out his free hand and stroked my cheek with his thumb. "You're pretty when you blush." This only succeeded in making me blush more.

His eyes drifted from mine, down to my lips. He met my eyes again and leaned slightly forwards. I had only kissed a few boys in my life thus far, and none of them even came close to this. It was like lightning. A warm light flowed through my body, and there was a tingling sensation that pulsed from my lips down to my fingertips. My body was humming again. Theo pulled away, too soon for my liking, but I was already breathless. Theo's eyes were glowing; he took a deep breath and pulled a little farther away. "Sorry to misbehave, but I couldn't resist."

"You don't sound sorry."

He grinned. "I'm not, not really."

"Me either." I was smiling too.

Theo glanced down, and then sat bolt upright. "What's wrong?" I asked. He seemed speechless. "Theo? What's happened?"

"Cassandra.... look!" He pointed to the bed. I sat up slowly and looked. Sitting next to where my hand had been was a small patch of blue wildflowers.

Theo gave a short burst of laughter, grabbed my face between his hands and quickly kissed me once more. "I told you before, I knew you had to be special."

Theo and I spent the next several hours talking while I tried to make things grow out of thin air. I was not upset that I seemed to have the most success when he was kissing me or holding my hand. I could tell he wanted more, but he respectfully held off and I was grateful for it. I had never had sex with anyone before, and while I wouldn't have minded with Theo, I still didn't want to rush things. I was drawn to him. I had never felt anything like it, and I wanted to explore these new feelings on my own terms. Finally, Theo grabbed my hand and told me to lie down. "It's close to dawn, we both need to get some sleep." He tucked me in against him, his arm wrapped around my waist. "Goodnight, Cassandra." He kissed me on my head and settled down. Within a few minutes, I had fallen asleep.

CHAPTER 10
-Theo-

CASSANDRA LAY THERE IN MY ARMS, BUT I COULD NOT FALL asleep. She was beautiful. As I traced a gentle finger along her brow, sweeping the loose hair that hung there and tucking it behind her ear, my mind began to recall every moment I had spent with her. When I'd tackled her in the grocery store, she had fought as hard as she could against me. The feel of her wiggling and squirming underneath me had brought my wolf to attention. *We have dominated the female! She is ours!* At the time, I scolded him, telling him this was not the time to be thinking of mating, that we needed to help Sebastian. My wolf was irritated, but he didn't fight me. Cassandra didn't stop struggling until the moment Sebastian knocked her unconscious. Doing so was unnecessary, and I'd told him as much, but he was furious that she'd gotten the jump on him. Izzy had taken the distraction as an opportunity and run, changing into her wolf form as she went.

Sebastian followed her and I stayed behind to deal with the girl who now lay at my feet, bleeding. *We need to help her,* my wolf whined. I bent down to roll her over. As I did so, I was struck by her simple beauty. Slightly on the shorter side, but slender and fit; her dark brown hair formed a halo around the porcelain skin of her face. My wolf must have taken control, because before I knew it I had picked the girl up. Her skin was like silk under my fingers. I took a deep breath, trying to breathe her scent in… something was wrong. I couldn't smell her. I tried again. Nothing. My wolf was confused and so was I. I tried once more, this time burying my face in her hair. I got something that time, but it was so faint. I closed my eyes and tried my best to concentrate.

Sebastian was a better tracker than I was, but having the girl in my arms and still not being able to catch her scent was baffling. I kept my eyes closed tight and placed my nose just behind her ear. *There…* It was still faint, but I could catch it. It smelled like nature, like being outside during a full moon run, or out in the woods just after a light rain. My wolf delighted in the delicate smell of her. I carried her back to the main house where my father questioned my decision to bring her with. I told him a half-truth, which was that I was curious about her, and I was, but it wasn't just her scent I was curious about. It was her. In the mere moments that I had seen her awake I could tell she was brave, and a fighter. And I knew the second I truly looked at her that her physical features were something to behold.

My wolf had not been happy with me for placing her in the cell in the basement, but I had to follow orders. This was where my father, the Alpha of our pack, wanted her kept for now. My inner wolf was agitated all night. *We should be down there with her.* I agreed, but I wasn't sure why. It wasn't like my wolf to become this attached to a female so quickly. At twenty-five years of age, I had had my fun with women, both werewolves and humans alike. I had known that my wolf wanted to settle down and start our own family and I was beginning to see his point of view. But this girl; this girl was different.

When I was allowed back into her cell, to bring her some food and warm water to wash the blood off of her face, I had to fight the urge to hold and comfort her. When she said it might have been better if Sebastian had killed her, I nearly shifted at the thought. It took every ounce of my will-power to keep my wolf in check at that moment. The next day, when she'd met the council, she'd held her own. She didn't challenge, but neither did she back down when the council and my father questioned and examined her. Walking her to the small guest cabin out front, I'd walked as slowly as I could to spend more time with her. Sebastian had looked disgruntled when I'd asked him to take her for a walk through the woods. I would have loved to walk with her myself, but I was curious, being familiar with the faint hint of scent she had, if I would be able to track her. To both my and my wolf's dismay and frustration, it was no use. I could easily pick up Sebastian's scent, but Cassandra's blended into the surrounding wood. Cassandra. Even her name affected me. At the thought of her my wolf's ears would perk up, his tail thumping and wagging.

The morning her friends had attacked, Sebastian had been on patrol. One of the other members of the patrol had been injured, but not seriously. I could never tell Cassandra that Sebastian was the one who had killed her friend. I could see the devastation his death brought her; it was written all over her face and her body posture. She would never forgive Sebastian if she knew, and I had to protect my brother. She had surprised everyone that day, by having the strength to stand up to my father. Doing so was not an easy task. Especially, when he was in a mood. I broke the rules that night by going to see her. I didn't know what to say, and I wasn't sure what this connection I had to her was, let alone knowing if she felt it too, but I had to go to her. I had to know that she was all right.

The day the witches took her, my heart stopped when I saw how stunning she looked. In my mind's eye I could see her, similarly dressed, walking down a wedding aisle towards me. My wolf was howling on the inside, agreeing with the daydream. I knew I could not stay away from her when the witches performed their ceremony. I did not entirely trust them, but it was what Cassandra wanted. When she fell into the river, I knocked two of them aside as I ran to her. She was all that mattered in my life. I knew, as I feared that she had died, that I loved her. The relief I felt when I could see that she was still breathing was indescribable. I didn't care if I was interrupting the ceremony or not. She was leaving with me. I would not leave her side again.

At some point my memories became a dream. I could see in vivid detail the vampire that had come into the room, hoping to hurt Cassandra. I knew what was happening thanks to the mental link the pack shared, and

I had stayed in her room in my wolf form, ready to die to protect her. The vampire, her fiery red hair flowing about her shoulders, beautiful but cold as stone, crept in. She wasn't prepared to find my wolf standing guard. I attacked without hesitating, but she put up a good fight. I could still feel her claws ripping into flesh, the ribs on my left side cracking – they would be healed by the following day. At one point she got close to Cassandra, and my wolf panicked. *Protect our mate with everything!* I launched myself onto the vampire, gaining a lucky bite right across her shoulder where it joined with her neck. I clawed her back to shreds with my paws until I gained enough of an advantage to rip her head off. I was shaking, and I could still taste the ash filling my mouth...

"Theo! Theo, wake up!" Cassandra was shaking me. I was drenched in sweat, but seeing her alive, lying next to me in bed spurred me. I grabbed her behind the head, rolled her over, and kissed her hard. She seemed surprised at first but then relaxed into the kiss. I groaned. Gods, she tasted good! I could feel her hips rise to brush slightly against me and my wolf growled his appreciation. "Theo..." She sounded so unsure. I stopped, pulled my lips away, and rested my forehead against hers while I calmed my breathing. What was wrong with me? It was not like me to lose control this way.

"It's OK, Theo. I'm OK."

I opened my eyes, and she was looking right in them. She placed her hands on either side of my face. and lifted her chin to kiss me slowly on the forehead. She then pressed my head gently down onto her shoulder. I was supporting most of my own weight on my elbows, not wanting to crush her. She was running her fingers through my hair, gently scraping her fingernails across my scalp and the smooth repetitive motion helped to slow my breathing. The blankets still lay between us; I had never crawled under them and knowing this also helped me regain my self-control. "Andie..." I wanted to apologize but she shushed me.

"Theo it's all right. I want to be with you. But not yet. I've never been with anyone before, and I don't want to rush it."

"Never?" I asked. I was surprised by her admission.

She shook her head, blushing as she did so. She was so beautiful when she blushed. I rolled to the side in order to take my weight off of her. Giving her a teasing look, I said, "Did you just 'shoosh' a werewolf?

She giggled. It was the finest sound I had ever heard. I nuzzled her neck.

"What am I going to do with you?" I whispered in her ear.

She giggled again, wrapping her arms around me.

"I'm sure you'll think of something." She whispered back.

My face broke into a wild grin as I jumped out of bed and ripped the blankets off of her, causing her to squeal. *Yes!* my wolf thought. He liked hearing her squeal in delight. So did I. I scooped her up in my arms and started to head towards the door.

"Theo! I need clothes!" She was right. She was in nothing but a pair of boy short underwear and a tank top. Anthea had placed the clothes on her before situating her in the bed. While I very much appreciated the view of her slender bare legs, the thought of the other male wolves seeing her in her underwear made my wolf bristle with jealousy. I set her down gently on her feet, kissed her chastely on the forehead, and told her I would be right back. I hated to be away from her for even a moment. I ran to the cabin outside and quickly located the blue sundress. I loved the way it hugged her curves, and the blue made her eyes stand out even more against her pale skin and dark hair.

When I came back, I had to keep myself from pouncing on her. Andie had thrown the curtains open, and the morning light was pouring in around her delicate frame, her underwear cupping her firm round butt cheeks. I allowed myself to enjoy the view for a moment before clearing my throat.

She turned and gave me a playful grin. "Put some clothes on Cassandra, before I change my mind and keep you in here all day." She grabbed the dress and sashayed to the bathroom. She was out in a matter of seconds. I grabbed her hand in mine and we headed out together.

As we stepped into the hall, Cassandra sniffed. "Coffee and bacon?"

The kitchen was far away, and I was surprised she picked up on the scent. I raised my eyebrows inquiringly.

"My senses have improved quite a bit since the nature ceremony," she admitted.

"Are you hungry?" Stupid question. She hadn't eaten in almost four days.

"Starving," she replied. We changed direction and headed to the kitchen. I was not surprised to find several of the pack members in there enjoying a late breakfast. Eggs, toast, bacon, sausage, and fresh coffee were all being cooked and laid out. Cassandra froze the moment we stepped into the kitchen. News travels fast and people were staring at her as soon as we walked in, causing the room to be shrouded in silence. Cassandra's face took on an odd expression, almost as if she were staring into the distance.

"Andie?" She did not reply but continued to stare into space, she was shaking slightly. As I examined her further, I noticed her eyes. Her pupils had dilated slightly, but the irises had changed. Instead of the usual bright blue, her eyes were filled with tiny electrifying lines of blue, green, and white. Her gaze flitted across the room, making contact with every person there. There was a funny sensation in the back of my mind, almost as if I were in my wolf form and another member of the pack were trying to reach out to me. Finally, her eyes turned to me. It was as though there were a direct line of thought going from my mind to hers and vice versa. Through her eyes, I could sense a mental connection with every wolf in the room at once, something I had only experienced in my wolf form. Goosebumps rose on my arms and my scalp and I felt chilled.

In a split second, everything went back to normal. The room was no longer cold, Andie's eyes were as they'd always been, and my head felt clearer than it ever had. All around the room, people were having the same reaction I was. Whispers started to occur all over the kitchen, and Cassandra looked terrified. I grabbed a plate, piled it with toast and bacon, filled a mug with coffee and grabbed her hand to take her back to the bedroom. She followed willingly. When we entered the bedroom, she sat on the edge of the bed immediately. "What was that?" I asked her.

"I'm not sure… It was like I was connected to all of you. I could see some of your memories; hear your thoughts. It was strange. And my body… it felt as if a small part of me had reached out to every one of you all at once, like my soul was being stretched a dozen different directions. It didn't hurt; in fact it felt good, like stretching tight muscles right after you wake up in the morning. That's the only way I know how to explain it…

"Theo, I'd like to try something, but I need your help. You're the only one I feel comfortable trying it with."

"What do you need me to do?" She asked me to grab a chair and sit across from her. I did and asked, "What next?"

"Just relax. Trust me." I did trust her, but it didn't keep me from being nervous as hell about whatever she was about to try. Cassandra locked eyes with me, and they dilated and lit up with electricity again. *Can you hear me, Theo?*

I could hear her voice in my head, but her lips had not moved. I tried to respond. *I can hear you.*

The corners of her mouth twitched in a small smile. *I want you to get up. Walk slowly outside the room. I want to see if I can keep the connection going even if I can't see you.* I did as she asked. I stood, and slowly walked out of the room, closing the door behind me. *Cassandra?* I tried to think the word her direction.

I'm here, Theo. It's much harder when I can't make eye contact but I'm here! I turned and ran back into the room. Cassandra was pale and sweating, but the look on her face was as though she had just won the lottery. "I want to try again"

"You need to eat first."

She looked displeased, but did not argue. She nibbled on some bacon and sipped the now lukewarm coffee. When the color returned to her face, she looked at me expectantly. "Can we go outside now?" This time, I was the one who didn't argue.

CHAPTER 11
-Andie-

I COULD NOT WAIT TO GET OUTSIDE. WHEN THEO FINALLY agreed to let me go, it was all I could do to keep from running. We had both been so surprised at what happened in the kitchen, and I was secretly ecstatic over being able to communicate with him through a mental link. When he was far away, or I couldn't see him it was harder, but I was learning, and I knew instinctively that it would become easier as I got used to my powers. We came to the end of the entryway, and Theo opened the door for me. My feet had barely passed the threshold when I became overwhelmed by the scene before me. Every color was more vibrant, every scent clearer and more distinct. I could smell each blade of grass, each leaf on the trees across the yard... I could even smell the water flowing in the river over a mile away. I could hear every creature moving, no matter how small, and if I focused hard enough, I could see them in my mind's eye. I took it all in. With every breath I breathed in, I could feel life filling me; it permeated every cell in my body. Theo was standing behind me and he placed a gentle hand on my shoulder. The physical contact with him caused a warm tingling sensation where our skin touched. I reached up and grabbed his hand, kissed it, and let it fall to his side. I turned my head forward again and took a step.

The moment my bare foot touched the earth, I could feel the energy of the entire planet pulsing through my body. With each step I took, the grass grew and small flowers of every kind appeared where, before, I would have simply left a footprint. I wanted to explore everything, to start walking in one direction and never stop. I started running, sprinting towards the trees. The feeling it invoked was like nothing I had ever felt. I was flying. My feet were hardly touching the ground. The feeling of the wind where it touched my bare skin was sheer ecstasy. I would have kept going forever had it not been for Theo.

"Cassandra, WAIT!" I heard him yell it both for the world to hear, and his thoughts echoed in my head, and I stopped just as I reached the tree line. I could hardly breathe I was so happy. My cheeks were flushed with excitement, and I thought I would burst from the pleasure I felt from being outside in the world.

Theo caught up to me, the look in his eyes one of awe. "Cassandra…." He fumbled for words. He shook his head and couldn't explain. *Show me.* I projected the thought towards him through our mental link.

The image of me taking my first steps onto the lawn passed before my eyes. I could see that I had been shaking slightly, that my breathing rate had increased. I could feel Theo's fascination and curiosity at the long grass and flowers I left behind with each step. When I watched myself start to run, at first I could feel the happiness Theo felt for me, but it quickly turned to fear and confusion. When I ran, I wasn't flying… I was disappearing! Parts of my body were flickering, first solid skin and then invisible. As I ran faster, more of me disappeared. Theo's fear had grown and he felt helpless, as though he were about to lose me forever and there was nothing he could do. It was in that moment that he shouted to me. I stopped running and my body pulled back together. The sight of me whole and in one piece had slightly calmed Theo's nerves, and I watched as he approached me in his memory. I was standing near a tree. As my hand reached out and touched it, my skin took on a bark-like appearance. Theo watched me lean against the tree and I saw myself, as he saw me now, half blended in with the tree bark, bits of moss and some small leaves growing in my hair.

I pulled back from his thoughts. "Did you see it?" he asked me breathlessly.

"Yes. Theo, it feels amazing. I can't even tell you how good I feel right now."

As I spoke the words I could see some of the concern and tension in his expression relax a bit, but then his face became very serious. "We need to speak to Anthea."

I had no intention of going back inside any time soon, and I could tell Theo would not leave me alone even for an instant. I pulled my body away from the tree and stepped closer to him, reaching for his hand. He grasped mine as if it were his life he was holding onto.

"Stay with me. Let me try to get her." I closed my eyes and reached towards the house with my mind – I could feel every being that was inside of it. I found the mind of one of the pack members that had been in the kitchen earlier. *Please do not be afraid. This is Cassandra. Please go find Anthea, the witch, and your Alpha, Roderick and send them outside. Theo and I will be waiting across the lawn.* I could sense that the pack member I had spoken to had understood, so I smiled kindly at Theo.

"Anthea and your father will be here soon."

I stood on my tiptoes and wrapped my arms around his neck. He responded in kind by wrapping his arms tightly around my waist. His lips brushed against mine. Everywhere he touched my skin, I could feel delightful shivers running from the point of contact to my spine.

"I love you." He had said it hardly louder than a whisper. I grinned broadly and kissed him hard on the lips. The love I felt for him was consuming me, and I was no longer uncertain of wanting that love. My doubts about him being a werewolf had vanished without me noticing. During that kiss, I had a vision of our future. I could see myself watching as a small boy, a carbon copy of Theo, ran playing around the yard with a little girl who had my chocolate brown hair. I broke the kiss and looked him deep in the eyes.

"Is everything all right?"

"It's better than all right. It's wonderful. I love you too, Theo."

We were still standing peacefully in our embrace when Roderick and Anthea found us. We broke apart, but continued to hold hands. "Please sit," I asked all three of them as I gestured to the grass. I found it easy now to command the attention of these powerful people. Even Roderick didn't argue at being told what to do. They all sat and looked at me expectantly. "I believe that when Anthea and the other two members of her coven performed the nature ceremony, that it unleashed more power in me than any of us could have predicted. What I have to figure out now is how to control it, and what to do with it. Roderick, you have been very kind to me thus far but I am afraid I must ask more. I would like to remain here for the time being, on your property." It was not really a question, but I waited for his response anyways.

Roderick looked at Theo and my hands, still twined together. "I suppose I will have to agree." He sighed.

"Good. There is one other thing I need from both of you. I would like to form a mental link to each of you. It won't take much, I simply need you to look me directly in the eyes for a few moments… This is not a request." I kept my voice even and calm, but put some authority into the words.

Roderick seemed to bristle slightly at the command and he huffed in frustration. "I am the Alpha of this pack. You do not tell me what to do on my land!"

"Father…"

"No! I have had enough of this *child* telling me what to do!"

Theo looked both furious and confused at his father's outburst, and I placed my hand on his knee to keep him from standing or shifting. *Don't move.* I sent the message to only him.

The sky above us started to turn grey. Wind whipped at our faces and howled in our ears. I gently placed my fingertips on the ground, and the earth around our little group split and cracked. Tangled roots covered in thorns began to shoot from the earth, twisting and turning and forming a wall behind me. My eyes never left Roderick's face.

"Enough!" Roderick shouted. His face was pale. The clouds above cleared. The roots stopped growing, bloomed some red roses and then all was still. The earth around us was the same as it had been, save for the large rose bush that now stood behind me. Roderick stiffened as he spoke again. "I will do as you ask." He sounded anxious.

Anthea had remained silent throughout the entire ordeal, but now she looked at me with a look of hope on her face, bowed her head and repeated the promise she had made once before. "Myself, and my powers are at your service," she said. She straightened and looked me directly in the eyes. It was not long before the connection had been completed. I now had access to every memory she had, and every spell she knew. I turned to Roderick. I could see on his face that he was still not happy, that he was furious I had forced his hand.

When I looked in Roderick's eyes, things were different. The connection was still there, same as the others, but every thought had a dark hue to it. It made my insides squirm, and my heart beat faster. I could feel anger flushing my face and the earth below me began to shake and tremble.

"Cassandra? Cassandra!" Theo's voice was working its way into my subconscious. I realized what was happening and pulled out of my mental connection with Roderick. The look I gave him was one of suspicion and betrayal; the look he gave back was one of fear and contempt.

Roderick stood up and without speaking a word, turned away and stormed back to the main house. Anthea stood as well. "I think, now that you can contact me whenever you need, it is time for me to say my good-byes." I nodded my head, stood and hugged her tightly, and sent her a silent, *Thank you*. She walked quickly, reaching the tree line just before she vanished into thin air.

I was exhausted. It was so difficult to sift through all of the thoughts and emotions I was receiving from everyone I had made a connection with. The emotional roller coaster I had been on since waking up yesterday had me drained and I still wasn't used to my powers or the effects they took on my body. I suddenly felt incredibly heavy. My arms and legs felt like iron weights and I wanted so badly to simply lie down and sleep. Theo bent, slipping one strong arm around my waist and placing the other arm behind my knees. Despite how heavy I was feeling, he picked me up and carried me as though I weighed no more than a feather.

"You need some rest." He mumbled quietly into my ear. I was so tired; I leaned my head against his shoulder and fell asleep before we even made it inside the house.

When I woke up, I was back in the bedroom where Theo and I had slept the previous night. I felt stiff and it was stuffy in the room. I stretched, making each muscle tighten and then relax. I rolled over and saw a note sitting on the pillow next to me.

I will most likely still be gone when you wake. I needed
to think. I plan on going for a very long run. Please try to make

yourself at home. Eat whatever you like from the kitchen. I'll be home soon. Try not to wonder too far without me.
Love,
Theo

The signature at the bottom made me smile. I had only known Theo for a few short weeks, yet our souls seemed destined to be together. The memory of the glimpse I had of our future made me smile wider as my hand instinctively went to my belly. I knew there was nothing growing there yet. How could there be? I mean, I was the daughter of Mother Nature... not the Virgin Mary. Realizing how hungry I was, I decided to head for the kitchen. I had eaten so little over the last few days, my stomach felt as if it were going to eat itself from the inside out. The house seemed relatively empty so I rummaged through the kitchen on my own, trying to find something that sounded good. I settled on a can of chicken noodle soup and a grilled cheese sandwich. My father had always argued with me that the only way to eat grilled cheese was with tomato soup, but I never did like the stuff... it always tasted like ketchup and water, mixed and heated to me. No thank you, I would stick to my chicken noodle. The meal made me feel more energized. I was anxious to get back outside and learn more about my new life.

It was late afternoon outside, the sky was overcast but still warm and pleasant, and the lawn was full of 'weres' meeting, talking, and having picnics. I made my way towards the tree line and walked only a few yards in, conscious that if Theo were to come back, I didn't want to go too far and worry him. I found a small clearing only a few meters into the woods. I sat with my legs crossed and closed my eyes. Breathing in the forest was like breathing in new life. It was a breath of fresh air filling my lungs after being suffocated by the walls of the big house. I hadn't even realized how uncomfortable my body had been inside the house until I had made my way back outside. I took a deep breath and tried to focus. I wanted to try and "feel" the weres I had made contact with.

To my surprise I could sense everyone I had made a connection with, as well as a few I hadn't. Apparently, as my body adjusted to my new powers, I was able to connect with creatures I had yet to meet face to face. Then something strange began to happen. The image of a perfectly detailed map of the entire area, filled with small glowing lights, began to form in my mind. There were a large number of them all clustered near each other and I realized it was right where the main house stood. I picked a light and tried to focus on that one only. Instantly, the picture in my head changed and it was as if I was both looking down on the scene in front of me, as well as looking through the eyes of the person I had contacted. I could both see a small child running from her mother playfully across the front lawn, while at the same time I could see from the small girl's point of view. I pulled back to the map with the lights. There were so many. I tried this time to reach out to all of them, and found it easy. I knew where every person was, what he or she was doing, and how he or she was feeling. My eyes snapped open and when they did, the connection was gone.

I decided to see if I could reach Theo. Since I knew his mind best, even though he was far away, I thought by now I would be able to find him with ease. I did find him, and I entered his mind the way I had entered the child's a few moments before. I saw both through his eyes and at the same time felt as if I were looking down upon the scene happening. My body became rigid and my heart froze. I could see what Theo was seeing, I could feel what he felt, and it terrified me.

CHAPTER 12

-Theo-

YEARS OF PRACTICE AND TRAINING HAD TAUGHT ME HOW TO be swift and quiet. Thanks to their scent and the mental link the pack shared when we were in wolf form, I knew the small group I ran with was not far behind. The acrid smell of death stung my nostrils and it filled me with rage. I had left the house, thinking I would go for a run. It would allow my inner wolf some time to stretch his legs after being confined to my human form for a few days, and it would give me the opportunity to think about where my relationship with Cassandra was headed. I had only run a few miles when I caught the distinct scent of a vampire. The bastards were on our land. The cloudy skies must have been blocking the sunlight enough to allow them out. Even with the clouds it was a risky move for any vampire. I reached through the link, sounding the alarm. There were three other wolves that had been near by on patrol, and they quickly changed their path in order to meet up with me.

As the smell filled my nose once more, I allowed the deep rumble of a growl to escape my lips. I pushed my muscles harder, ignoring the burning sensation that came from my legs as I picked up my speed. My wrists and ankles screamed in protest as I skidded from a full out run to a dead stop. Something was wrong. The trail we had been following for the last twenty miles had suddenly gone cold. I backtracked a few steps. The vampire's scent was there, but there was a clear spot where the trail seemed to just disappear. I reached down my mental link, projecting my confusion to the others but I received no response. I tried again and was met with an empty darkness. As the feeling of dread grew in my stomach, the hackles between my shoulder blades rose.

I counted quickly as they dropped from the trees surrounding me. I could take one, maybe two, by myself, but there was five. It didn't matter. As long as I was breathing I would try and kill as many of them as I could. I didn't hesitate. I attacked first, lunging at the nearest vampire. I managed to take him by surprise and ripped his head clean off before the next one tackled me. I couldn't help the yelp of pain that escaped me as I felt several ribs crack. I wiggled free of the vampires grasp, struggling to take a deep breath as I did. Another one of them landed on my back, using their razor sharp nails to rip the side of me open. Hot blood oozed down, drenching my fur and the ground beneath me.

I flung myself sideways, managing to pin the vampire that had been on my back between myself and a tree. The large pine nearly cracked in half from the force, but the vampire seemed merely stunned for only a second. It was all the time I needed. I whipped around, landing my teeth perfectly just below where the head and neck met. With a sickening squelch I ripped the head from its body. Two dead. Three more to go.

The remaining vampires all formed up in a line, and as I turned to face them I could feel my legs shaking underneath of me. The mud beneath my paws and the dizzy feeling in my head gave testament to just how much blood I had lost from the gash in my side. The vampire in the middle stood, he began to laugh. It was a laugh you picture your favorite horror movie villain making when they finally have their victim cornered. The way he laughed caused a tinge of fear to run through me before I truly began to panic. I couldn't see. It wasn't the blood loss either. It was as if a cloud, dark and stormy had been pulled over my eyes. Not long after my sense of smell and my hearing left me as well. I was left, lost in a world with no sights, no sounds, no smell and no way to get out. It was then that I heard a steely voice echo through my head, "*Make her come to us.*" It was followed by a softer voice, one I recognized.

"*I'm Coming Theo.*"

"*No, Cassandra….No…*" But I knew in my heart, even if she heard me, she wouldn't listen.

CHAPTER 13
-Andie-

MY EYES BURST OPEN AS I FELT THE POWER AND MY BODY'S natural instincts take over. What felt like hot electricity pulsed down each nerve, causing me to tremble. They had taken Theo, and thanks to my new internal map, I knew exactly where they were. *Time to test my strength* I thought as I started to run. As I picked up speed, it began to feel less like running and more like flying. I became the wind. My body was no longer solid as I passed through trees and bushes as if they were no more than air.

As I traveled swiftly towards Theo and his captors, I reached out with my mind to Anthea hoping that with all of her wisdom she would know the kind of power that overtaken Theo. Anthea's answer was swift and full of warning. Only powerful, dark magic could have caused what happened to him. She urged me to stay away but I shut her out. I was almost there, and I would not abandon Theo.

A few minutes later I arrived in the small clearing where Theo had been ambushed. The three vampires jumped into a crouching stance, clearly having been surprised by my swift arrival.

"Where is he?!" I demanded

"Where is who?" A pale almost sickly thin blonde vampire answered me in a high-pitched, falsely sweet voice.

"Do not play coy with me. Where is Theo?"

"Oh him….yes, well, he is nearby. But he certainly wont be *around* much longer. Oh well, he played his part. He got you to come here." A sneer appeared across her face as she continued to speak. "You don't look all that special to me," she mocked. "By the way, we have someone here who wants to meet you." She stepped aside and gestured behind where her and the other two vampires had been standing. There was a figure there, it was female, but she looked more ghost than human. She was consumed in a dark billowing cloud that moved with her as she came closer. She spoke in the same steely voice I had heard inside of Theo's head.

"Hello Cassandra. So you are the one my race is calling the *surAvani*. I expected…more."

The insult didn't faze me as I locked my vision onto the dark pits that were all that remained of the witch's eyes.

"Expect away." I retorted.

Just as my body and my instincts had led me here, they now told me what to do. I managed a deep breath, the air passing my lips just before a bright beam of light shot from my chest. As the light struck the dark cloud surrounding the witch, her screams began to fill the wood. Screams that told me, the witch was now burning to death from the inside out. I continued to focus my attention in her direction until, in a final burst of light, the witch, and the tree that had been directly behind her, exploded. The witch was now gone, but the tree had simply been shattered into a hundred pieces. The wooden shards flew like bullets through the air. Two of the vampires burst into ashes as long splinters pierced their hearts. The third, the unlucky blonde who had mocked me earlier, was merely injured as dozens of smaller wooden splinters logged themselves deep into her skin.

My hand twisted and another large tree next to her began to grow. The trees branches began to twist and turn until the vampire was ensnared. Each arm and leg was pulled until she was suspended spread eagle in the air. Two final branches twisted their way towards her. Each ended in a razor sharp point, one below her and one above. The end result was that every time the hardly conscience blonde took a breath; the branches would pierce her skin just above and just below her heart.

With the last vampire effectively subdued, I reached out mentally to feel for Theo. My instincts led me to some thick bushes only a few feet away. He was mostly hidden by the bushes, and was still in his wolf form. His fur was matted with wet dark blood and his breathing was shallow and ragged.

A few howls sounded nearby, but I knew help would not arrive soon enough. I grabbed the scruff of his neck and struggled to pull his weight out from under the foliage. Now covered in dirt and Theo's blood, I tipped my head towards the heavens. *Please let this work*, I prayed. I placed my shaking hands back onto Theo's listless body. Clouds the color of dirty melted metal began to form and swirled perilously above. With a brilliant flash of lightning the rain started, heavy and punishing drops that fell from the sky drenching me in a matter of seconds. I took another deep breath and closed my eyes. As I did, I could feel Theo's soul trying to leave him. I reached out, clinging to it with everything I had.

Time halted, and a light, softer and gentler than the one that had escaped me when I attacked the witch, started to seep from every pore of my body. Its warmth surrounded me, and I slowly opened my eyes. The raindrops, which had been so unrelenting before, now hovered midair like crystals hanging from invisible string. A frozen bolt of lightning lit the sky, casting strange shadows across the forest. The glow surrounding me started to move, taking with it, its comforting warmth. It moved down my arms, and settled inside of Theo's chest. I could feel the cold raindrops splashing across my face once more before the world turned black and I collapsed on the ground next to Theo.

CHAPTER 14

When I came to, I was so tired I couldn't even open my eyes, so I tried my best to listen. Moans and gasps of pain came from the still bound and injured blonde vampire, but the reassuring sounds of heavy breaths were coming from Theo. One of my hands was still clinging to his side, the soft fur warming the skin of my palm. There was another sound, one that took my brain a moment to recognize. It was the sound of several sets of heavy paws running towards us. When the witch had died, the spell she had cast to take away sight, smell and sound must have broken, releasing the other wolves Theo had been traveling with from its grasp. Within moments the sound of the running wolves reached us and a voice I now recognized well spoke out.

"Get them out of here. Send more of the patrol to meet me here. The vamp is injured, maybe we can capture her and get her back to the house alive for questioning." It was Sebastian. I wanted so badly to ask him how Theo was, but all I could manage was a quiet moan before arms I did not recognize picked me up and began to carry me.

By the time we reached home, I was more alert. I had slept for most of the journey, but had woken up long enough to ask the man who carried me a few questions. I learned his name was John, and when I asked him about Theo, all he could tell me was that he was alive. When we finally made it back, instead of taking me to the main house, John carried me to a building I had never been in before. It must have been some sort of sick ward, because the moment the door opened the smell of antiseptic and bleach filled my nose. John insisted on carrying me all the way to the bed, even though I knew he had to be tired from our long hike back. He set me down gently before quickly excusing himself.

A quick glance around showed a tall slender woman with a kind face walking down the rows of beds towards me.

"Where is Theo?" I asked the question before she was even able to introduce herself.

"Dr. Nelson took him to the back room to examine him. My name is Olivia, you can call me Liv if you like. Now sit back dear and let me check your vitals."

I did as I was told. My stomach was in knots, but the knowledge that Theo was alive and with the doctor receiving the help that he needed helped to ease the worry that had been tightening in my chest.

"Your vitals are all good." Liv smiled warmly at me. "Your blood pressure and heart rate are up just a tad, but it sounds like you all went through quite the ordeal so I'm not surprised. You look awfully pale though… I'm going to start an IV to give you some fluids and then I just want you to rest."

"But Theo…" I started to argue with her.

She placed a hand on my shoulder. "I promise I'll update you as soon as I know something." She started my IV, tucked me under the blankets of the small uncomfortable hospital cot, and bustled away.

It wasn't long before Dr. Nelson came out of the back exam room. He spoke quickly to Liv, who pointed in my direction. Dr. Nelson then hurried over. He pulled a chair up to my cot and sat down. "Hello Cassandra. My name is Dr. Nelson. I'd like to ask you about what happened if you feel up to explaining it to me."

I nodded. I told him what I could remember of the fight Theo had with the vampires, and about what I had done. He seemed stunned at first, but then he placed his weathered hand on mine and said, "If only I could replicate what you have done. You saved his life. The vampire that ripped his side tore clean through the muscle. Even with the quick healing power of wolves, he would have bled to death. Instead, whatever you did stopped the bleeding, repaired the muscle perfectly, and left only a slight scar on his skin. He will be tired I am sure for a few days, but he is awake and getting dressed now. I insisted he let me talk to you first, not an easy argument to win I might add…" He smiled and winked at me. He then gave me a quick physical exam, agreed with what Olivia had done, and added that he would like to see me eat something before I left the infirmary. After leaving my bedside, he went back to the exam room, opened the door, and allowed Theo out into the ward.

Theo's face was drawn and pale, his long stride carried him to my bedside in a few easy steps. He sat on the edge of the bed, lacing one hand behind my neck and grabbing my hand tightly with his other. He bent and brought his forehead down to meet mine. "What on Earth were you thinking? You could have been killed! I was so worried about you… I tried to tell you not to come…" I kissed him. His mouth covered mine, his fingers gently gripping the hair at the base of my skull. He needed me, and I needed him. We broke apart, both breathless, and sat still holding onto each other that way for several minutes.

Liv cleared her throat. "Sorry to interrupt, but Doc wants you both to eat." Theo and I both sat up and Liv placed a large tray of food on my lap for us to share. "Doc also says he would like for the two of you to stay the night for observation." She blushed slightly as she told us, "And I'll have no hanky-panky in my ward. You will sleep in separate beds."

As she walked away, Theo winked at me and said, "Let's see her try and put me in a separate bed." I giggled and the sound seemed to relax him.

We spent the next hour picking at the food and talking about what had happened. It was clear now that the vampires had laid a trap. When attacking me at the house hadn't worked, they decided to try and drive me out into the woods. It worked, except they didn't win the fight. They clearly thought that the dark witch who was helping them would be strong enough to fight whatever powers I might have. They had been wrong. While the fight had drained me of my energy, the witch's powers had been no match for mine, and she had been relatively easy to dispose of. I told Theo how amazed I was at what I could do. That I was learning more and more about my strength and myself every minute. It scared me a little.

After we were done with the food, Liv took the tray away. With the freed up space, Theo climbed into the bed with me. Liv looked at us from across the ward and pursed her lips but said nothing. Theo and I lay quietly for a while, enjoying the feeling of being wrapped in each other's arms, and taking comfort in the fact that we were both safe and together.

Theo was gently stoking the hair on my temple when he spoke softly. "I never thought I would love someone the way I love you, Cassandra. And I certainly never expected to feel this way about someone so fast. When I knew you were coming but I couldn't stop you, couldn't protect you... I've never been so scared in my life."

My head had been resting on his chest and I tilted my head back so he could see my face when I spoke. "I feel the same way about you, Theo. When I saw what happened to you, I could feel your pain, and I wanted to destroy the thing that made you hurt so badly. You're right; this *has* all been very fast, but it feels right and I wouldn't want anyone else standing by my side as I tried to figure all of this out." He tucked his knuckle under my chin, kissed my nose, and squeezed me a little tighter.

The door to the infirmary opened and a gust of cool evening air came in. Sebastian walked down the aisle to the bed Theo and I were curled up on. He took the seat that was still by the bedside and looked at his brother. The stress he was feeling was clear on his face. His jaw was clamped tight, and his brow lined with tension. His dark hair looked as if he had been running his fingers through it a hundred times. He took a deep breath and rubbed his knees with his hands. "Brother, we have a problem." He glanced at me. "I think it would be better if you heard this as well, but not here, we need to go someplace more private." I could feel Theo's muscles tighten under his clothes. He got up out of bed and walked to the desk Liv was sitting behind, said a few quick words to her, and returned. Liv followed, looking disgruntled, with some gauze and a roll of tape. She clamped my IV off, took it out, and bandaged my arm where the needle had been inserted. When she was done putting the bandage on, she stormed off in the direction of what appeared to be Dr. Nelson's office.

Theo looked at me. "Can you walk?" I nodded and stood up. My body was still tired, but the food and IV fluids had helped.

"Follow me." Sebastian led the way out of the infirmary, and started to walk towards a small building that was directly behind it..

Theo slowed his steps. "No, Sebastian, we can find somewhere else." I looked between the two men.

Sebastian gave me a sad and apologetic look, something I was not used to seeing from him. "I am so sorry Cassandra, but it needs to be in here. It will not be pleasant for you, but it is important that no one overhear us."

I was confused. "What is this place?" Neither of them could look me in the eye… Sebastian cleared his throat and, staring at the ground, told me it was a small morgue. My heart ached. The only person I might know who would be in a morgue was Rory. I had never gotten the opportunity to truly say goodbye to him, and I guess no one else had had the time to bury him. I swallowed hard and gave a small nod to Sebastian. He opened the door and the cold air of the morgue hit my skin. We all stepped inside as Sebastian switched on a dim light. It was freezing in here. Along the back wall was an old cot where a thin sheet covered what I knew was Rory's body. I walked over. Rory didn't deserve to be in this place. He hadn't deserved to die. He had been my best friend for twenty years. I felt ashamed that I had not thought more of him the last few days. I turned to the two brothers who were both giving me as much space as they could in the tiny room. They were both standing with their hands clasped behind their backs and their heads slightly bowed. "I'd like to give him a proper funeral. Can I do that?"

Theo stepped forwards and wrapped me in a hug. "Of course you can. We'll do it tonight, OK?" I nodded into his chest, choking back some tears that were forming. I broke away from Theo, wiped my eyes, and looked at Sebastian expectantly.

Sebastian seemed uncomfortable. He was fidgeting and seemed nervous.

"What's going on Sebastian?" Theo asked.

"You won't like it. Hell, I hate it. But you're Beta, and my brother; I had to come to you! But if it's true Theo, it's bad… really bad."

"Well, what is it?"

"It's about that vampire bitch we captured. I've been trying to interrogate her for hours now. She wouldn't give up much at first, but I made her talk…" Sebastian was pacing back and forth in the small room, raking his hands through his hair again. "It's like this… I wanted to know why they laid the trap. Whatever vampire created the trail we followed knew they were risking a lot coming so far into our territory alone. Why would they do that? I finally got the answer. They wanted Cassandra. We thought they had found out about what Andie is thanks to Izzy, but that was all wrong. I went to the cell she was in, there is no air vent that leads to the council room, so that was a lie…" He was rambling and making very little sense. Sebastian took a deep breath and looked at Theo. "Theo, I think it's Dad."

CHAPTER 15

"You think what is Dad?"

Sebastian took another deep breath, puffing his cheeks out as he slowly blew the air out of his lungs. "I think Dad is the one giving information about the pack, and about Cassandra, to the surrounding covens. Not Izzy."

Theo was speechless for a moment, but when Sebastian's words finally sunk in, he looked furious. "You are wrong. That is our Alpha you're talking about!"

"I know, Theo, but please believe me, all the information points to him."

While slightly shorter than Sebastian, and not as broad, Theo's dominance was clear. His stance and facial expression, his tone of voice, it all caused Sebastian to back away, slumping his shoulders as he went. "Take me to this vampire. Now!" He stormed out of the tiny morgue, slamming the door open on his way. Sebastian and I followed. As I closed the door I looked back at Rory. The thought that I would put him to rest in peace soon was a small comfort.

Once outside, Sebastian took the lead. We headed into the main house, back to the basement, back to the first cell I had been held in. Only when we walked in, most of the sparse furniture had been removed. The bed was gone and the vampire had been strapped to the only remaining chair in the room using metal chains. There were angry red welts on her skin where the chain rubbed and I noticed that each link had a cross emblazoned on it. She hissed and bared her fangs like an angry cat when we entered the room. Sebastian and Theo both stood over her with their arms crossed over their chests.

"Tell him what you told me," Sebastian told the woman. She grinned and spat on him. The saliva sizzled when it hit his skin and he quickly wiped it off. He backhanded her, and though her head snapped to one side she merely laughed.

"Is that all you've got, pup?" Both men were shaking with anger and hatred. I stepped between the two of them, and, placing a hand on each of their shoulders, told them to let me talk to her.

"No. It's too dangerous." Theo said.

I looked up at Theo. "I'll be fine. And you'll be right here to protect me if something goes wrong. So will Sebastian." I turned my head to look at him and Sebastian nodded. Considering that, since my arrival, Sebastian hadn't been the most welcoming towards me, he seemed slightly surprised that I had put my faith in him to protect me. They both stepped back to allow me more room.

"What is your name?"

"Why? Want to know who to blame when I kill your man? I'm going to enjoy ripping his throat out." There was a cocky one-sided grin on her face.

"No, but I would rather you simply told me instead of having me force it from you."

She laughed out loud this time. "Ha! That's rich coming from a puny thing like you. What are you anyways… they never did tell me."

It was my turn to smile. I could feel my eyes change and my body begin to hum once again. "I'm someone you really don't want to mess with…"

I locked my eyes with hers and was immediately sucked in. I could see everything in her memory from the day she'd been born. Who she was, the face and name of the leader of her coven… I could see every kill she had ever made. Delving through her memories made my skin crawl. She was evil. Her soul was dark and twisted and I wanted to stop but I needed more information. *Show me.* I knew she heard the command inside her head. I could tell she was trying to fight me, to fight the light I brought into her darkness, to fight the connection I had made with her. I ended the connection the moment I had the information I needed. It was going to kill Theo to hear the truth. I pulled back and could feel the cold, evil sensation leaving my body. The warmth of the room was starting to seep back into me and I was grateful for it. The look on the woman's face was sheer terror. She had not liked my presence in her head. I walked slowly across the room. I tried not to think of what I was about to do, but it needed to be done. I grabbed something off of the table that I assumed had been placed there on purpose and walked back to her. She had a single red tear of blood sliding down her cheek. "Please…" It was all she said before I plunged the wooden stake into her heart. For a split second she froze in a silent scream before she burst into a cloud of dust. The chains that had restrained her fell limp around the chair. Her name, I had learned, was Jessica.

CHAPTER 16

THE TWO BROTHERS WERE STANDING THERE WITH THEIR mouths hanging open. I looked at Sebastian first, then Theo, and walked out of the room. They followed without speaking. The three of us walked in silence until we were back in the morgue. I shut the door behind us before turning to talk with them. They both looked as if they were going to burst with questions but I held my hand up to silence them.

"Please, let me ask a question first and then I will explain everything I learned." Neither of them said anything so I took their silence as my answer. "I would like to know what happened to your mother."

They were both taken aback and confused by my question, but it was Theo who answered. "Our mother was a very dominant female. She was third-in-command next to my father and his last Beta. She was in charge of organizing and running all of the patrols of the area. There was a vampire scent that was caught by someone who was new at patrol, so he told Roderick. Roderick decided that he, his Beta, and our mother were to try and follow the scent, and hunt down the vampire if possible. When my father came back he was badly injured, and he was alone. He said that they had chased the vampire all the way up to the edge of a ravine on the far side of our territory. He said when they got there they were ambushed by a whole group of vampires. Our mother had been attacked by several of them at once and had died trying to fight them off. The Beta was knocked over the edge of the ravine cliff. Roderick barely escaped with his life."

I let the silence sit for a moment before grabbing his hand. "I am sorry you lost your mother, and I am sorry for what I am about to tell you. Your mother, Rebecca, and your former Beta, Michael, were indeed killed in a fight with vampires, but it was not how your father described. The vampire I just killed, she was there and I saw the truth in her memories. Your father set it up. He was worried your mother and Michael were becoming too dominant, and he was suspicious that the two of them were planning a mutiny. He made a deal with the vampires to lay a trap. The vampires set a trail that led to the ravine and when your parents and Michael arrived at the designated spot, your father turned against your mother and Michael to help the vampires kill them. Since then, he has been paying his debt to the vampires by selling valuable information about your pack and others. In return, the vampires keep their silence, and are prepared to help take down anyone your father sees as a threat to his position as Alpha. That now includes both me and you, Theo." Disbelief was written on both of their faces, and my heart broke for them. "I am so sorry." The words were not enough to express the heartache I felt on their behalf.

Thirty minutes later, the three of us still sat in the tiny morgue. I stood behind Theo, my arms wrapped around his waist as he and Sebastian discussed everything we had just learned. At first they had both been stunned at the news, then angry at me for saying such things about Roderick, then angry at their father for betraying their trust; both as family and as pack leader. Now, they were as stumped as ever about what to do. It is against werewolf nature to go against the Alpha, and both men were struggling to the core about how to proceed.

"There's no other way around it, I'll have to do it." I had been too busy thinking about everything to realize they had come to a decision, but the sound of Theo's sad yet determined voice caught my attention.

"You'll have to do what?" I asked.

"I will have to challenge my father for the position of Alpha."

"Oh! Well, that shouldn't be too bad, should it? I mean, you are younger and stronger than him."

Both Theo and Sebastian looked at me with grave eyes. "Cassandra, it means I will have to fight my father... to the death." Theo could hardly whisper the words.

"I really hope you are right about this Andie, because if your not, then I will have not only have committed mutiny, but the murder of a family member for no reason."

My arms dropped from around Theo's waist. His words had sent sharp stabs at my heart. But while his words had hurt, I knew he had every right to question me. He had a lifetime of trust built up in Roderick, whereas he really hardly even knew me.

Sebastian walked over and clasped his brother in an embrace of reassurance. They both seemed like they were about to cry, but heaven forbid the world ever see a male werewolf cry, especially ones as dominant as these two, and in front of a woman!

Sebastian gave me an awkward hug as well before departing. Once he was gone I turned to Theo; the beautiful, strong, dominant werewolf I had managed to fall in love with in only a short period of time. I placed my hands on either side of his head, tipping his face down towards mine. "What can I do?" I wanted so desperately to help this man who had become more important to me than life itself. Theo simply shook his head. This was a mission he had to do himself. "What if I lose you?" Just the thought of losing him was enough to bring tears to my eyes and make my chest ache.

Theo's chilly demeanor from moments ago warmed and he kissed me deeply, his eyes blazing. "You will never lose me. You and I are meant to be together, always." The way he said it made me believe him without an once of doubt.

"When will you do it?"

"Soon… but not tonight. Tonight, we have other things that need to be taken care of." He nodded in the direction of Rory's body, and my heart sank again. Rory deserved so much better than this. I swallowed hard and gave a small nod. Theo walked over to him, removed the thin white sheet, and gently picked Rory's body up in his arms. He looked so pale, not like my Rory at all. I missed him so much. Despite all of the recent changes in my life, Rory had been home, or at the very least a reminder of home, and now he was gone from this life forever. I opened the heavy metal door for Theo and followed him out across the lawn.

We walked for probably two miles. I hadn't noticed how large the compound was. Behind the main house there were several other small houses and buildings, and farther out was a small church. The outside of it was small and quaint, white with blue shutters. Theo continued to walk around to the back, where there was a small, secluded graveyard with a large oak tree near the edge. "We don't have occasion to bury our members often, but when we do, they are buried here." It was a beautiful area. The graveyard looked out past the grand oak to a large field of wildflowers before turning into more wooded hills. The gentle light from the moon made it very peaceful. There were only a dozen small headstones marking the place where someone that had once been loved was buried. I chose the next open plot and Theo lay Rory next to it. While it filled my soul with sadness, a part of me was thankful that I was the one to put Rory to rest. Theo had offered to go grab some shovels but I told him there would be no need. A simple motion with my hands and the dirt lifted up in one giant lump. Another gesture and the earth settled down into a pile nearby. Theo, once again with a tenderness that surprised me, climbed into the hole, lifted Rory down, and placed him with his arms crossing his chest. Theo climbed out, kissed me on the temple, and took a few steps back. He was giving me my space to grieve, while staying close enough if I needed him.

I stood over the grave and began to cry, large tears streaming down my face uncontrollably. "I will miss you forever and always. You were my brother, my best friend. You were my family and I will never forget you." I stood there a few more minutes, weeping over the loss of my closest friend and the last connection I had to my old life. I lifted the pile of earth into the air once more and settled it as softly as I could over Rory's body. I placed a hand on the freshly turned pile of dirt and as I did, a beautiful bush covered in red roses grew out of the ground. This would have to be his grave marker. Better these beautiful flowers than some cold piece of stone with a few dates carved into it.

I collapsed on the ground and began to sob again. Theo sat down with me, placing a leg on either side of me and wrapping me in his arms. It wasn't long before I was sitting on his lap, my face buried in his chest. His t-shirt became damp where my tears had soaked into the fabric. After a while I finally stopped, and Theo kissed the tip of my nose. "I'm sorry this had to happen, Cassandra."

"Me too. I will miss him so much. He never even knew that I've changed, what I've become. I'll never get to share that with him."

Theo kissed me again, this time on the cheek. "Would you like to stay a little longer?"

"No, I don't think I could stand to cry anymore."

We stood together, and with one last look at the grave that now belonged to my best friend in the whole world, we started to walk away.

CHAPTER 17

Theo led me, hand in hand, back to the main house. Lost
in my own thoughts I hadn't realized what he was planning until we arrived
in the bathroom of the room we had stayed in previously. He let go of my
hand and started to fill the tub with hot water. He even scrounged under
the sink and found some scented oil that he added to the water. Taking a
bath had been the farthest thing from my mind a moment ago, but now
the idea of soaking in the hot water sounded like the best possible thing.
I suddenly felt very grimy and dirty. I hadn't bathed since the night of the
nature ritual.

Theo set out a towel and made for the door. "I'll be right out here if
you need me."

I'm not sure what made me decide to say it, but I didn't want him
to go, not after everything that had happened. "Theo, will you get in with
me?"

His breath caught in his throat and the look he gave me had my knees
feeling like Jell-O and my stomach muscles clenching. "Are you sure?"

I flushed bright red and could barely squeak out the answer that yes,
I was sure.

Theo stepped back into the bathroom, shutting the door behind him.
He walked over to the tub and turned the faucet off. The tub was steaming
and the water smelled like lavender. He grabbed the hem of his shirt and
pulled it above his head. As he did, my eyes traced down his body. He had a

pronounced collarbone that led to strong pec's with small brown nipples on them. Down further I could trace every muscle along his sides where they wrapped around his ribs and met with a very defined six-pack. It ended with a light trail of hair leading from his belly button to a delicious-looking V encased by snug jeans that hung perfectly on his hips. My mouth was suddenly dry, and I was nervous to take my own dress off.

"Come here, Cassandra." I obeyed. I wanted to be closer to him, to touch him and make sure he was real; not just a perfect creation of my imagination. I was inches from him. I reached my hand up to press it against his chest and he caught it in his own hand. He brushed his lips across my fingertips and told me to turn around. Once again I obeyed. His voice was deep and gravely and his eyes were shinning – I could tell his wolf was close to the surface. I turned around and when I was facing completely away from him he stopped me. He brushed my hair over my shoulder, exposing one side of my neck. He then clasped the small zipper in his strong fingers and started to pull it down. As he did so, he ran light kisses from the back of my ear to the tip of my shoulder, pausing only to suck lightly on my earlobe. I watched him in the mirror as he undressed me. The sight of him slipping his hands under the shoulder straps of the blue dress and pulling it down to expose my bare skin had me feeling hot all over. I could feel my body start to hum again.

Theo walked around me slowly. His stare made me want to cover myself back up, but when I tried to hide he stopped me. "No, Cassandra. You are stunning, let me look at you." His eyes drank me in. He bent down and began to plant more light kisses on me. This time he started with my lips, then trailed along my jaw line, down to my collarbone, and finally locked his lips around one of my nipples. I almost shouted in pleasure. He was sucking at it, causing my nipple to harden and become even more sensitive. He reached a hand up and began to lavish my other nipple with his hand, rolling it between his fingers and pulling at it. Not hard, but just enough to send shock waves through my breast and down to my nether parts. Despite having underwear on I could feel myself getting moist between my legs. I was disappointed when Theo stopped. He stood, grinning like the crazy sexy wolf he was and raised an eyebrow at me. "Your turn." His eyes were shining and his pupils had dilated. His straight nose flared every time he took a breath. I reached with shaking hands and traced, with the lightest touch I could, the same pattern that he had kissed on me. I continued down his stomach, letting the muscles ripple beneath my fingertips until finally my fingers were running across that delightful smattering of hair and across his waistband. His eyes were closed, his head tipped slightly back, and he was trembling. I took a small step closer to him. While my hands clumsily tried to undo his jeans button, I returned the favor and began to suck on his nipples. When I gently grated against them with my teeth I was rewarded with a low rumbling growl from his chest.

Having finally gotten his button undone, and pulled down the zipper, I slid a thumb under the waistband of his jeans and boxers on each side of his hips and gave a small tug. His pants came down just enough that his erection sprang free. I stepped back a few inches and stared at him. While I had been breathing rather heavily before, now I was practically holding my breath. Theo could tell my nerves had started to act up again. He came to me, grabbing my face between his palms. He kissed me, gently stroking the inside of my mouth with his tongue. After a moment he broke away. "Cassandra, are you sure? I don't want to force you into anything you don't want to do."

"I'm sure. I want this. I want you." I uttered each statement between breaths. Theo pulled his jeans off the rest of the way and before I could even think, he had scooped me up sideways and was carrying me back into the bedroom. He lay me down on top of the soft comforter and climbed on top of me. He kissed me once more before exploring lower with his lips and returning his attention to my nipples. When he had me writhing and arching my back, trying to push more of me into his mouth, he stopped and went lower still. He allowed his tongue to taste all over my stomach, and nipped lightly at my hips. He slipped his fingers though the sides of the underwear I was wearing and gave a deft pull. They slid down my thighs and Theo continued to pull them down and off completely. He looked at me again, his eyes begging for permission and I gave it willingly to him. His mouth covered my lower lips, his tongue circling my clitoris and gently sucking at it. My hips shot up, pressing me harder against his jaw, and my mind went blank. Its only focus was Theo's tongue and the pressure it was creating deep inside my belly. My fingers and toes curled as Theo continued to pleasure me. He stopped just long enough to tell me that if he hurt me, to say something. I could barely nod my understanding. I wanted him to continue. There was a deep primal need within me that needed him to keep going. Theo ran two fingers down between my legs, feeling the moisture that had gathered there and gently pressed them inside of me. It was a shock at first, but as he moved his fingers within me, stroking places I hadn't even known existed, my body became more comfortable. The pressure inside my belly was no longer a pressure; it was a coil, wound so tight that I was desperate for its release.

Theo stopped suddenly, leaving my body desperate and hungry for more. He got on his knees before climbing next to me. His position as he moved gave me a good look at his swollen manhood. My breath caught in my throat. I wasn't sure he would fit!

As he lay down next to me he reached over and grabbed my hand, placing it on his lower stomach. He was asking, not pushing, letting me take control. I slid my hand down his stomach until it came in contact with the base of his member. It was a strange feeling, gripping him hard in my hand. The skin was smooth as silk but underneath felt hard as rock. The instant my hand closed around him Theo gasped and his breathing quickened. I ran my hand up and down him, exploring the feel of him and his size. It didn't take long before Theo flipped me back over, placing himself on top again. He was lying on top of me, cradled in between my legs, but supporting all of his own weight. "I need you, Cassandra."

Hearing the words come from him was all the courage I needed. "I need you too." He locked his mouth on mine and slowly lowered his hips. He was as gentle as he could be. When he first pushed inside of me he went slow, allowing my body to adjust to him. I could hear him panting in my ear, trying to maintain his control. Each time he would pull out, the next time he would push a little deeper. It was exquisite. My whole body was winding up tighter and tighter. My fingers dug into Theo's back, spurring him on to start moving quicker. The feel of him stretching and filling me had me moaning with each thrust. Each time he entered me he would rub against a spot inside that sent jolts of pleasure throughout my whole body.

He was still supporting most of his own weight on his elbows, allowing me to arch my back. It allowed him to go just a fraction deeper inside of me, and it also put my nipples back in range of his mouth. The feeling of him sucking and pulling at my nipple while still pulsing inside was enough to push me over the edge. The coil that had wound so tightly inside of me snapped, and all of the pressure came flooding out. My muscles clamped hard around Theo, and the pleasure caused me to scream. Theo groaned, pushed inside of me twice more and then with one final thrust came as well.

We both lay there panting, wrapped in each other's limbs, trying to catch our breath. Theo nuzzled the nape of my neck, kissing me gently and causing my skin to raise with goosebumps. I could feel the rush of air against my neck as he took a deep breath. Immediately after doing so he propped himself up on his elbows and looked around the room before bursting into laughter. A deep, happy, cathartic laugh.

"What's so funny?" I knew I was new to this whole sex thing, but I was pretty sure laughter was not the response you were hoping to get from your lover once it was over.

"Cassandra." He was speechless, and gestured to the rest of the room. It was completely overgrown – it looked as if a tropical garden had exploded into life inside the bedroom. Plants and flowers covered every flat surface, and ivy hung from the ceiling lamp and draped across the curtains. I gasped and covered my mouth with my hands. I hadn't even realized I had made anything grow, I was so focused on how Theo was making me feel. He laughed again and pulled me into his arms. "I think, the next time we have sex it will just have to be outside." He winked at me in response to my embarrassed grin.

"Come on beautiful, let's go actually take that bath." Theo headed back into the bathroom, and I could hear him adding a little more hot water to the slightly cooling water. I quickly got rid of the overgrown foliage and followed him. I walked in just in time to see him sitting down inside the full tub. He looked at me and cocked his head slightly to the side, like a puppy, waiting for me to join him. I stepped in, careful to step in-between his legs and not on them. He held my hand, keeping me steady as I lowered myself into the hot water. It took a moment to get used to, but once I adjusted to the temperature I relaxed and leaned against Theo.

"Hold still…" Theo said. He had a strange look on his face but I did as he asked and held still. Theo scooped some water in his hand and slowly emptied it, dribbling water down my neck to my shoulder until it finally ran off my collarbone back into the tub. The warm water felt good and so I closed my eyes, but Theo's amused laugh made me open them again.

"What?" I asked him.

"Watch." Theo took my arm and placed it so my hand was just under the surface of the water. "Move your hand, slowly." Again I did as he asked and this time huffed my own amusement. The water moving across the surface of my skin had the same effect the wind did. My skin took on the appearance of rippling water and my hand seemed to all but disappear.

I turned around to face Theo and the two of us acted like small children playing in the tub. For the next half hour, we entertained ourselves by causing the water to move across my skin in one way or another and marveled at the result. When the water began to cool and our fingers were pruned, we decided to get out. Theo wrapped a large fluffy towel around me and kissed me on the forehead.

As we dressed I expressed my confusion over my newfound heritage. I knew nothing about nymphs, and therefore nothing about being one. Theo offered that there was a small library next to the entertainment room.

"It has a small section on some supernatural history. It isn't much, but we could take a look, try and do some research.." The idea excited me and we agreed to grab a snack from the kitchen on our way to the library.

We browsed through the several shelves of books while snacking on some reheated leftovers we found in the kitchen. We finally selected three books that looked like they might hold some answers. A few hours later I had a more basic understanding of what I was. We learned from a mythology book we had pulled that nymphs were considered either lesser gods, or spirits of nature. What had really been interesting to learn was that the nymphs the books referred to all only represented one aspect of nature: trees, water, wind, animals, etc.

The nymphs of the Old World were said to be full of life, extremely nurturing, and very fertile. The last bit of information had me blushing deeply and Theo grinning wickedly at me. Nymphs did their best to nurture and protect anything belonging to nature, but specifically the part of nature they represented. What had me most excited in our research was what we found about their appearance. All nymphs, in their human form, were said to be beautiful young women, but when placed in their natural surroundings, could transform at will and take on the appearance of the part of nature they were most closely linked to. For instance, a tree nymph could turn into a tree, water nymphs could all but disappear when placed into a lake or stream, but most importantly, the animal nymphs could take on the physical attributes of the animals they protected. Anthea had said I was the daughter of Mother Nature, and the most powerful nymph there was.

We already knew that I could make things grow (or un-grow) on command, my body could take on aspects of wind, water, and the bark of a tree… did that mean I could turn into an animal as well? Could I transform into a wolf like Theo?

Just the thought of it had me chewing on my nails; a nervous habit I hadn't done since I was a kid. Less than a month ago I had still been just plain old Andie. Now, I had more power than I knew what to do with. Theo gently grabbed me by the shoulders, kissed my forehead again, and said, "It's late. Why don't we go to bed?" I nodded my consent, knowing it would be hours before I would be able to fall asleep.

Instead of leading me to the guest bedroom we had been using, Theo led me upstairs. Opening a door, he informed me that this was his room. It wasn't as big as the guest suite downstairs, but I felt more comfortable in here. The bed frame was rustic wood, and the light greens and browns the room was decorated in reminded me of nature. There was a large bay window with a sitting bench that offered a nice view of the woods. His room was neat and organized and there was a bookshelf that held everything from science fiction to books on history and government. Theo walked to a large closet and came out with a button up shirt and handed it to me to use as a nightgown. After having sex and taking a bath together, I no longer felt shy about him seeing me naked, so I changed in front of him. Theo watched me and as I was buttoning the last button he stepped closer, scooped me up, and placed me on the side of the bed. Standing between my legs with my arms around his shoulders, Theo inhaled as he ran his nose from behind my ear, down my neck, to my shoulder. "You are too attractive for your own good, did you know that?" I had time to respond with a giggle before he kissed me deeply. By the time he stopped kissing me I was slightly short of breath.

Quickly, he kissed me once more, walked to the small attached bathroom, and stripped down to his boxers, tossing his dirty clothes into a hamper. He brushed his teeth and closed the door for a moment of privacy before offering the use of the bathroom to me. When I came back he was already lying under the covers. I crawled in next to him and he quickly pulled me close. Spooning me, he whispered in my ear, "Goodnight, my beautiful Cassandra."

Despite everything that had happened and everything that was weighing on my mind, I fell asleep quickly. It felt as if I had barely shut my eyes before we were woken suddenly. The door to the bedroom had flown open and Theo responded by shifting instantly mid-leap off of the bed. His growl quickly died when he saw three members of his pack standing in the doorway.

"You have both been summoned to present yourselves to the council immediately." The three remained standing in the doorway, waiting for us to move.

Theo changed back into his human form and answered in an angry tone that made the hair on my arms rise. "No need to escort us, we will get dressed and be downstairs momentarily."

"I'm sorry sir, our orders came directly from the Alpha."

A deep growl resonated from Theo's chest. He grabbed clothes for himself as well as a pair of sweatpants and a tee-shirt for me to wear. I went to the bathroom and changed quickly. We followed our guards out the door. I was confused, but I could feel the anger coming off of Theo in waves. With orders from the Alpha or no, his wolf was not taking the challenge the guard gave him easily. I could see his wolf eyes shining and could sense that he was barely maintaining his human form.

When we entered the council room I noticed that Theo became stiffer, more alert. It did not take me long to realize almost the entire pack was in the room. It was dead silent. Through my newfound connection with the pack I could tell that there was a wide range of emotion filtering through the group. Anger, confusion, fear… It was difficult to focus on anything but the mass of emotion I was feeling. Theo grabbed my hand and walked us to the dead center of the room, standing directly across the council table from his father.

The sight of Roderick sitting at the head of the council, as Alpha of this pack, with the knowledge of what he had done made me sick and angry. I could tell Theo was feeling the same.

"Cassandra, as Alpha of this pack it is my duty to inform you that you are no longer welcome here. Your presence has become a danger to my family and I will not have you on our land. You are to leave this place, alone, never to return. If you do, I have issued an order for your execution on the spot. My son is to remain here, and is forbidden henceforth to see you."

My heart froze with ice and fear. Leave Theo… I couldn't. I couldn't handle this without him. He was the only person I loved left alive. I looked at Theo's face; his eyes were glowing once more, and every muscle in his body was quivering.

"No." Theo's answer rang with such a dominant force across the room that almost everyone lowered his or her eyes to the ground. Everyone except Roderick and me.

"Excuse me?" Roderick sneered. "I am not only your father, I am your Alpha. You will do as I command or you both will be executed." This sent a few quiet murmurs across the room. Most Alphas would die to protect any member of their pack, and Roderick had just threatened to kill his own son.

Theo stood straighter, lifting his chin slightly as he looked Roderick right in the eye. "I challenge you for the position of Alpha over this pack and this territory. You are not worthy of the trust and power bestowed upon you."

The hall erupted with gasps and small cries. A fight to the death is what Theo had told me. He would have to either kill his father, or his father would kill us both. It felt as if my heart had fallen out of my chest. I had all the faith in the world that Theo could win, but I knew it would not be an easy fight.

Roderick's face had turned purple with rage. "Outside." The word was barely audible through the growl that ripped from Roderick's throat.

In only a few minutes, the entire pack had moved outside to the front lawn. Early morning light filled the air and the grass was still damp with dew. A large circle was cleared in the middle of the spectators and both Roderick and Theo stood near the center. My nerves were on fire; I was frantic. I didn't know if I could watch Theo battle to the death. He took his shirt off and quickly kissed me. "I won't let him hurt you. No matter what."

Without another word he turned back to face his father and transformed into his wolf form. Roderick took his own shirt off and I was disappointed to see how strong and fit he was despite his age. Roderick gave a short bark of laughter before transforming into his wolf. My breath caught in my throat. I had seen Theo and Sebastian and plenty of the other pack members in their wolf forms, but nothing had prepared me for seeing Roderick. His wolf was impressively large, bigger than any I had seen before, except for maybe Sebastian's. He was grey, with black markings across his back and on his legs. But it wasn't his size or color that caught me off guard, it was his scars. The light pink tissue lacked any hair and cut from high on one shoulder across his chest and down to his belly. There were several more small scars that dotted his sides and the back of his neck. I could not imagine the injuries that would have been severe enough to leave those kinds of marks on a werewolf. They must have been deadly to have left a mark at all.

Theo stood ready, his hackles raised, his teeth bared. Roderick looked at him and his wolf seemed at ease, he almost looked as if he were smiling, excited for the fight. He lowered his head slightly, placing his body into a crouching position, growled once and sprang at Theo. My heart jumped out of my chest as the two collided. Claws slashed and teeth flashed. They began to roll about, fighting for the upper hand. The noise alone was enough to frighten anyone. My ears filled with the sound of snarling and growling. Suddenly, I heard a loud yelp and I couldn't breathe. The two broke apart, both with their sides heaving from exertion. Roderick was panting heavily but I could see brighter red dripping through Theo's russet-colored fur on his side. He was shaking, but his eyes were trained on Roderick. I started to step forward. I had to help him, I couldn't let him do this!

Someone grabbed my shoulders and held me back. I struggled to throw their hands off when Sebastian gripped me tighter, saying, "He has to do it alone." His voice was tight with fear and worry, mimicking my own feelings. Roderick flew at Theo again, and this time I forced myself to watch closer, to see every move.

Roderick had Theo on the ground, but Theo threw him off using his hind legs. He whipped around and grabbed Roderick by the scruff of his neck and shook hard, causing blood to start dripping from the base of Roderick's neck. Roderick threw himself onto his back, crushing Theo beneath him and breaking free. While Roderick got himself up, Theo snatched his hind leg in his jaws and with a sickening crunch, clamped down on Roderick's leg. Roderick howled in pain. This time when they broke apart, both were bleeding and Roderick was limping badly on his hind left leg. It was Theo who attacked first this time. I begged in my mind to let it be over, to have Theo win. It was killing me to stand here and watch him fight. Blood stained the grass red all around them as both screamed and growled and yelped in pain. The fighting lasted only a few more minutes. Theo had Roderick pinned, his jaws wrapped tightly around Roderick's neck. With one quick jerk he could have torn his throat out. Another moment longer and he would have, but Roderick rolled his body slightly, showing his belly to Theo, and whimpered pathetically. Theo paused, but didn't let go. I could hear Sebastian release a deep breath behind me and I knew the fight was over. No one was dead, but Roderick had clearly surrendered. He whined again, and Theo growled once before letting him go. Theo took two steps back and stared Roderick down. Roderick kept his eyes on the ground and rolled over so that he could crawl towards Theo.

Nobody expected it, and it happened so fast. Roderick had crept towards Theo on his belly, begging for mercy, before standing and slashing at Theo's face. A split second after the surprise attack, Roderick turned tail and ran. Theo let out a howl and charged after his father into the woods. Three others, including Sebastian, turned into their wolf forms and followed suit. Even on three legs Roderick was fast, and thanks to his dirty move, he had a head start. For over an hour we sat there, waiting for news, for a sign, for anything. Thanks to my abilities I knew that the group following Roderick were safe. While I continued to track their whereabouts in my mind, I refused to delve into their thoughts, not sure if doing so would distract them.

Finally, one of the women from the pack approached me. She was middle-aged and though appearing quite shaken herself, she offered to take me inside and make me some tea. I nodded, not really hearing her, and followed her to the kitchen. We sat in silence while she made tea for several of the pack who had come with us. I quickly learned that her name was Martha. She was a mid-ranking wolf in the pack, but had been Michael's wife before Roderick had killed him. Although, she still did not know his death was at Roderick's hands.

With nothing to do but wait, it wasn't long before the handful of pack members that had come to the kitchen began to talk. I listened quietly at first.

"I just don't understand. I've known Theo since he was a boy, it's not like him to challenge out of the blue for Alpha. And Roderick has always been a good Alpha to us…" It was Martha. My heart ached for her. She had spent the last two decades thinking vampires had killed her mate. In reality, it had really been the man she called her leader and she was sticking up for him at this very moment. I learned quickly that the entire pack was feeling unsettled due to the challenge and the change in leadership. Hearing that there had been a change, that Theo had indeed won, settled some of my nerves, but knowing he was still out there, hunting Roderick down had me chewing my fingernails again. Martha came over and placed a warm hand on my shoulder.

"Don't worry, dear. Theo will be fine. Now that he is Alpha, someone in the pack would know if something were to seriously harm him."

"Has he sent a message to anyone through the pack link?" I asked, desperate for news.

"Not that I know of. But…" She hesitated before continuing. "If something were to happen that caused him to loose his status of Alpha, the pack would have felt something." I understood her delicately worded message. Theo wasn't dead. I already knew that much, but hearing it from someone else still helped to ease my nerves. I resisted the urge once again to reach into Theo's toughts. I looked at Martha, at her round kind face and kind smile and once again I was filled with sadness on her behalf. There hadn't been time before the challenge to let the pack know what was really going on, but now seemed as good a time as any, even if it did weigh heavy on my conscious to have to be the one to tell them.

"Martha, will you sit with me please?" I asked her, reaching my hand out for her to grab. She looked surprised but took my hand in hers and sat down next to me anyways.

"I am so sorry Martha."

"For what dear?" Martha asked quizzically.

I squeezed her hand, took a deep calming breath, and closed my eyes. I located every ball of light that was a pack member in my mental map. While I could see the group traveling with Theo, I quickly blocked them out, effectively preventing me from seeing through their eyes, and preventing them from being distracted by the message I was about to relay. I called upon the mental link I now shared with the pack and recalled the story about what Roderick had done to Theo's mother and to Michael, his former Beta. I revealed his dealings with the vampires and with the other surrounding packs and covens. I also informed them of my deepest regrets at having to burden them with this new information, but thought it was only fair they knew the true reason Theo had challenged Roderick. When I finished and opened my eyes it was to silence and stares from every pack member in the room. Martha still held my hand but her eyes were filled with tears and I was unsure if the look of hatred on her face was directed at myself or at Roderick. I hoped it was the later.

There wasn't much talking after that. Several of the pack members sat for a few hours in the kitchen, sipping tea and eating some snacks that Martha laid out. Over time more and more trickled out, returning to their own homes. Martha stayed with me until I felt a nudge at the back of my mind. It was Theo. He was OK and was on his way back home with the other three. They had been gone all day and it was already near sunset. My body relaxed and I finally felt able to breathe again. I passed the message on to Martha. Having heard that the new Alpha was on his way back, she excused herself, tears starting to form once more in her eyes, and told me if Theo needed her when he arrived, she would be at the cemetery where Michael was buried.

Having no words of comfort to offer her I nodded my understanding before she left. I hated what the pack had to suffer today, but at the same time I felt a justice had been done. One of their own had been betraying them for years, and Roderick had finally gotten what he deserved.

Several more hours passed before Theo actually made it home. When he did, he found me in the kitchen, cold cup of tea in front of me, head down on the kitchen table, and sound asleep. I awoke to his gentle caress across my shoulders and his warm arms picking me up.

"You're home," I mumbled as I nuzzled my nose against his chest.

"Yes Cassandra, I'm home." I could hear the slight smile in his voice.

"What time is it?" I asked.

"It's after one in the morning."

He carried me across the threshold to his bedroom and lay me on the bed.

"What happened?"

His voice sounded sad and angry at the same time when he replied. "I'll tell you all about it tomorrow. Get some sleep."

My body and mind were exhausted and my nerves were fried from worrying about him all day. When he crawled in next to me and once more tucked me into his arms I felt safe and comfortable. It did not take me long to fall back asleep.

CHAPTER 18

-Theo-

THE MOMENT I HAD MY FATHER BEAT, I COULD FEEL IT. THE change in power, the change in myself, the instant connection with the rest of the pack; their thoughts and feelings, I could feel it all. With my jaw still clamped around his throat, my wolf had urged me to finish the job, to make it so he could never challenge us for rights to the pack again. But my human half saw his submission and recognized it as a chance to keep my father alive, to not have to kill him and live with the guilt. A lot of good it did me. The moment I let my guard down, Roderick took advantage and tried to blind me. He'd aimed badly – he cut me across the face but missed my eyes before he turned tail and ran. With his injured leg healing fast and his momentary head start he had a decent lead on us. I took after him and knew from my connection with the pack that Sebastian and a few others had shifted and were following to help bring him back. It was useless. We ran all day, following his trail. His direction made no sense. It seemed as if he had no idea where he was headed and kept turning back the way he had come only to zig zag and turn back to his original direction. We followed him all the way to the farthest edge of our territory where his scent disappeared. I was furious. My wolf was even more so, and livid with me for not finishing Roderick off when we had the chance.

Sebastian's wolf paced back and forth at the spot where the trail met the edge of our territory. I could tell he wished to pursue them further, but I commanded him to stay within our boarders. To my frustration, Roderick was gone. God help him if I ever saw the man I once called father again.

Shortly after turning towards home I sent a message to Cassandra, hoping she would get it. She acknowledged my message with one of her own letting me know she had broadcasted what Roderick had done. I was secretly grateful that she had taken that burden from me. I could tell by the emotions the pack was feeling that they wholeheartedly supported my challenge after learning of Roderick's betrayal. I was Alpha now… I only prayed that I was worthy of the position. I loved my pack and would do anything to protect them, and Cassandra.

It was after one by the time I crept back into the main house. I could smell Cassandra in the kitchen and I walked there quietly. Pausing behind the door I listened carefully. There was no sound save for the steady breathing of a single person. I opened the door and found Cassandra asleep, face gently resting across her arms, which were folded on the table. Her brown hair looked as if she had been running her hands through it all day. My fingers twitched, wanting to do the same thing. I gently tucked a loose strand of hair behind her ear and she stirred. I picked her up. She was slender, with just the right hint of feminine curves. The memory of her body pressed beneath mine was enough to make my passion stir, but tonight was not the night. I wanted to hold her, to know that she was safe. Tonight was time for me to reflect on everything that had changed; tomorrow would be a very different day.

The next week flew by in a blur. I was Alpha, and the pack and their safety were now my responsibility. The pack needed stability, so my first order of business was to find my Beta. I was pleased when it turned out to be Sebastian. There was no need to fight to the death when determining rank: our six most dominant wolves were asked to shift into wolf form, where they would stare each other down one by one. If a challenger lowered their eyes, breaking the eye contact, it was a sign that they were a less dominant wolf. Therefor the winner would be determined by his or her ability to maintain eye contact with the other five challengers. More than once I had to intervene to prevent fights from occurring but overall it went very smooth. Sebastian would make an excellent Beta. He was fiercely loyal to the pack and strong enough to maintain control and order, but deep down was reasonable enough that he would listen to anyone with concerns.

I hated being away from Cassandra, but if Roderick was on the vampires' side, she was in grave danger. He knew our land and our defenses better than anyone. My only hope was that the combined power of the pack, and Cassandra, we would be able to protect everyone.

Since my time was preoccupied with pack business, in an attempt to help keep Cassandra busy, and hopefully help her train and hone her abilities, I sent a message to the witches asking for their assistance. Anthea seemed rather shocked at the invitation I sent her, but accepted willingly. I had invited her and the other two witches who had performed Andie's ceremony to temporarily move into some of the small cabins in the woods off of the main house. Cassandra could then freely spend time with the witches learning and training, without having to be too far from my protection.

When I asked Cassandra what she thought of the idea, she had bravely put on a smile and thanked me. I could tell she was scared, and nervous, but she never ceased to amaze me at how well she was handling everything. So much had happened to her over the last few months, and she had taken it in stride, never faltering in her ability to take on a new challenge. I had never met anyone like her.

While her days were spent in the woods nearby with the witches, mine were spent managing pack business as well as leading constant patrols. I had doubled the border patrol, even going as far as to in-list volunteers to help fill the shift needs. The entire pack was working together, and it made my chest swell with pride to see them band together. The connection I now felt with every pack member was indescribable. They were all relying on me, and I would not let them down. I only wished I could hear and feel Cassandra the way I did them. Only when she opened her connection to me could I feel her, read her thoughts. She could keep the connection open, but she could also close it on demand.

I bet she would not close it if we were mated. My wolf pouted. A part of me wondered the same thing, but how to ask her? And would she feel the same? When a pair of wolves mated, they became bonded for life, not only through their commitment, but through magic as well. Once mated, a pair of werewolves become so in tune to their partner, it was as if they shared one soul. Thoughts and emotions could be shared even in human form, and the thought of mating with another became an unthinkable act. It was very rare that a wolf chose to bond with a human. When this did occur, the bond created by magic was still there, but weaker than that of a wolf-to-wolf bond. But Cassandra did have magic in her veins. *How would she be if we were mated and bonded?* I wanted her desperately, and for life, but would she want me?

CHAPTER 19

-Andie-

I WAS HAPPY TO HAVE ANTHEA, FLORENCE, AND DOROTHY back with me. While Theo and I had continued our research as best we could about my ancestry, the witches were a much bigger help when it came to learning about my abilities. So far I had simply let my instinct take over. Each day I spent with them was split in two. The first half of the day was spent learning to control my powers. At first, it took all the mental power I had to channel my power where and how I wanted it, but with each try it became easier, until it was almost effortless. The afternoons were more exciting. After the witches let me break for lunch and a rest, we would experiment, testing the limits of my powers and what I could do with them. It turned out the All Mother had not been stingy when she gifted me. What I had discovered on my own and with Theo was nothing compared to what I could do now. I had not shared much with him, wanting to surprise him.

After a week of spending every day with the witches, even they began to be out of their depths. My powers had expanded beyond what I could have ever imagined. Anthea however, was convinced a small part of me was still holding on to my connection to my human life, and once I let that go, my powers would be even greater. As it was, my powers already allowed me to connect with the entire planet. Every living creature and plant, I could feel and access their energy. I could control the weather, I could make anything grow from nothing, or make it wither back into nothingness. Like the nymphs of old, I could transform my body. I could now turn myself into a tree, dive into a stream and disappear with the current; I could travel with the wind above the clouds. In the rare time I had alone I had been working on shifting into a wolf. I did not want anyone to know before Theo did.

At the end of each day spent with the three witches, I was drained. Theo had given Martha the task of ensuring that I kept up with daily activities such as eating and bathing. Most nights I was asleep in our bed before he even came home, and was too far gone to even wake when he crawled in next to me.

To everyone's disappointment there seemed to be only two limitations to my powers. One, while I had been able to connect with the vampire we had captured by staring directly into her eyes, I could not locate any of the vampires on my mental map. Because the vampires weren't technically living, I could not connect with them the way I did the rest of the world to find out what they were doing, or where they were hiding. Second, I could not find Roderick either. While there was the small chance that meant he was dead, Anthea seemed to believe that the vampires had found another dark witch who was hiding him with a spell. I checked multiple times a day, trying to locate him, but only succeeded in frustrating myself.

Theo and I had hardly seen each other over the last week, and I missed him terribly. Hence it was much to my surprise when I awoke one morning to find him still in bed next to me, fast asleep. A lazy smile drifted across my lips before I looked at the alarm clock. The neon green 11:00am had me rolling over to shake Theo before jumping out of bed. I had my shirt on inside out and my pants halfway up to my knees before Theo grabbed me and pulled me back onto the bed.

"Theo! I'm going to be late meeting Anthea! I can't believe this! I know I set the alarm…"

"Relax, Andie. I turned the alarm off. I told Anthea that I needed you today."

My heart stopped racing and my body calmed. He needed me. And I had a day off from the witches and magic training!

"I can't believe we slept so late…"

"I instructed Sebastian to cover for me. You and I both clearly needed some rest. Besides, I have some plans for us today." That sly grin was back on his face.

"What kind of plans?"

"The kind that starts with this…" His lips found my earlobe and began sucking gently. At the same time his hand found the hem of my shirt and his fingers drifted softly across my stomach. A warm feeling flooded me. We had not had sex since the night before Theo became Alpha, and I was eager to experience it again. His lips traveled down my neck, barely touching my skin, but the sensation had me tilting my head to give him better access. His hand roamed from my stomach to my thighs, his fingers brushing along the inside of one before moving to the other. I groaned slightly and lifted my hips just an inch, hoping his hand would travel just a little further to the apex of my legs.

"You have far too many clothes on my dear." His deep voice sounded husky and had me desperately reaching to pull my shirt up and kick the pants I still had wound around my ankles off. The moment my breasts were bared his mouth locked onto my nipple, which shot a jolt straight between my legs and my back arched, trying to push myself farther into his mouth. He didn't stay there long. His mouth drifted down, trailing kisses along my stomach, until he reached the barrier my underwear provided. With no effort at all he grabbed them and ripped them to shreds. I was now completely exposed to his direct line of sight. It made me blush and squirm slightly, but then his mouth continued its administrations and finally made contact with the part of me that was aching so desperately for his touch. I panted and pushed my hips forwards again. Every muscle in my body was trying to tighten, and my whole body flooded with an aching need. His mouth alone was enough to have my body twitching and me groaning in between gasped breaths, but he didn't stop there. Focusing his mouth on the sensitive nub between my folds, Theo slid his fingers next to his mouth and eased them into me. I could hear him growl his pleasure at how wet I was. It was excruciating pleasure, the way his tongue and fingers worked together. Pulsing, rubbing, licking… my body was bucking with its need to release. Theo's fingers moved faster and my body was wound so tightly I lost track of everything except what he was doing to me. Finally, my release tore through me, sending every muscle spasaming and my lungs struggling to draw breath.

While still in a haze I looked at Theo. His eyes were blazing with his wolf showing through and his canines were slightly extended. Oh my! He was stiff and ready. The sight of him on top of me, every muscle in his chest and abdomen chiseled and flexed, the tantalizing V formed by his hips that joined at his long and thick staff, had my stomach clenching in anticipation once more. With a swift yet gentle motion he slid his arm under one of my legs, lifting it until it was almost hooked over his shoulder. He pressed forward, sliding into me, filling me slowly. He then withdrew and then advanced pushing deeper inside me once more. By the third time he withdrew and pushed forward I couldn't breathe. I gasped and begged him for more. My fingers were laced through his hair and I pulled his face closer until his ear was right next to my mouth.

"Please…" It was all I could manage to whimper. Theo growled and I could hear his breath becoming more and more ragged as his pace increased. His free hand was massaging my breast and lightly rolling my nipple between his thumb and forefinger. My need for release was building again. A strange sensation of tightening and climbing all at once. Every muscle in my body longed for more. I whispered my plea once more in Theo's ear and he responded instantly. He was pushing deeper and harder than I thought possible, but it didn't hurt. Quite the opposite. It had me screaming and arching my back in pleasure, and my body clamped down hard around his. Every muscle inside of me was locked as I screamed, intense pleasure pulsing from between my legs to every nerve in my body. With my release Theo found his, grunting my name as he came.

We lay there, panting and trying to catch our breath. Theo had his forehead resting on my chest near my collarbone. He lifted his head and kissed me affectionately before taking a quick glance around the room.

"Well, the room survived," he said with a wink. It made me giggle.

"The witches have been teaching me how to control my powers better."

Theo's face suddenly became very serious. "Good. Controlling it will help…" I could tell his thoughts were turning to the ongoing concern of Roderick and the vampires.

I grabbed his face and made him look at me. "None of that. Today is about us and rest. You said so yourself." He grinned, kissed me once more, and jumped out of bed to get dressed. I stretched languidly before getting up, my muscles feeling pleasantly relaxed. After getting dressed, Theo grabbed my hand and we headed downstairs. The main house was busy and we ran into several of the pack on our way to the kitchen. When we entered, the kitchen buzzed with people and we saw Martha ordering them about. Theo cleared his throat loudly, surprise on his face.

Martha came bustling over and addressed us both. "I'm sorry, I hope you are not angry. Sebastian said you had wanted to have a nice lunch so Andie could get to know more of the pack, but they all want to get to know her as well, so I've turned it into a barbeque out on the front lawn." While waiting for our reactions, she bit her lip nervously.

I was beginning to greatly care for Martha; she had shown me so much motherly affection over the last week I could hardly deny her this. I smiled and thanked her while giving her a huge hug. "Barbeque sounds wonderful!" She beamed at me and then glanced at Theo.

"If she's happy, I'm happy. Thank you, Martha. It smells wonderful, when do we eat?" he asked with excitement. Martha relaxed and said everything was almost ready. She handed us each a dish to take outside and shooed us out the door.

I must have been tired to have slept through all of the noise and commotion going on out on the front lawn. Most of the pack was there, setting up picnic tables and spreading paper place settings. The tables were already weighed down with food and my mouth watered at the sight and smell of it all.

"How did she just 'throw' this together?" I asked in astonishment.

Theo laughed. "It's not hard to get wolves together quickly when food is being offered. For a while after my mother died, Martha sort of took over the planning and cooking for everything that was going on at the Alpha house." His face turned grave. "My father said it was too much for him, having Martha there filling my mother's position, so she moved out of the main house…" He took a deep breath and smiled, returning his beautiful and strong features to a happy expression. My heart ached for him. I knew what it felt like to lose both of your parents, but I couldn't imagine the torment Theo was feeling for running his father off. Betrayal or no, Roderick had still been his dad.

The early afternoon was spent pleasantly, eating until I felt like I might burst and meeting new faces. I had seen most of the pack at some point or another, but never in one place. It was comforting for them and their inner wolves to get to know me, as it didn't appear I was going to be leaving anytime soon. It was also comforting for me to put a face and a person with each of the tiny balls of light that I could sense when I closed my eyes. I found myself being drawn to the younger children more than I would have in the past, their free spirits and innocence filling me with joy. I felt happy here, and safe, things I had not felt in a very long time.

When the sun started to descend in the sky Theo pulled me away from the group. "I thought we could go for a hike. There's a beautiful spot with a small lake I don't think you've seen yet, it's not too far. We could make it there and be back around sunset." He seemed nervous but I couldn't figure out why. I told him the hike sounded wonderful with one alteration. I had him start us off in the right direction and shortly after getting into the woods had him stop. We were deep enough into the woods now that we could still hear the group on the front lawn, but not see them.

"I have a surprise for you…" I told Theo as I started to take my clothes off.

He growled and prowled over to me, grabbing me around the waist. "I like this surprise," he said.

His gravelly voice had me blushing but I gently pushed his arms down and stepped away. "That's not the surprise." He looked confused and maybe a little hurt that I had pushed him away, but the expression didn't last long. "I thought instead of hiking to the lake, maybe we could run there instead?"

"Run naked? I don't think it will be too comfort—" He stopped mid-sentence and his eyes got wide as he watched me change. The transition was still difficult, but change I did. I had practiced for days, and finally my last few attempts had been good and I was happy for the chance to show Theo.

"Cassandra…" He was speechless.

I knew what he would see – I had been happy with my appearance as a wolf as well. I had a lean muscular frame, my coat was white, almost silver, my only markings the black tips on my ears and the dark lining around my eyes.

I gave him a moment to adjust and then huffed at him as I took off running in the direction we had been headed. It took only moments for him to catch up, and his wolf tackled me playfully. We rolled a few times, nipping at each other's necks, his wolf intent on smelling me. I held still and let him explore every inch of me. After a few minutes he licked my face, let out a playful bark, and took off running again. I followed, pushing the muscles in my legs. I had always loved running as a human, but running as a wolf was something completely different. The angle at which I saw the world, the millions of scents and sounds I never would have noticed as a human, and my increased agility made it incredible. I pushed harder and picked up my speed. Theo noticed and picked up his as well. What would have been an almost hour-long hike took us fifteen minutes to sprint.

We arrived at the lake breathless, our sides heaving. Theo ran straight to the edge of the water and began playing at the shore. His hind end up and his front end down, he yipped at me to join him. The cool water felt good on my heated body. We both drank deeply from the lake before Theo caught me off guard and tackled me sideways into the water. It was only a few inches deep, but it was enough to have my coat dripping and heavy with water, so I stepped out and shook. Theo followed me and we both changed back to human form. I had hardly a moment to look at him before Theo collided with me once more. This time however, it was not to play.

His chest pressed against mine and he quickly bent, grabbing me under my buttocks and picking me up so my legs were wrapped around his middle. He pressed a burning kiss to my lips and I could feel his erection just below me. He took a few quick steps in the direction of some soft grass nearby and lay me down. As wonderful as the morning had been, this was better. It was slow and passionate. Theo would bring me just to the brink before pausing his motion, allowing me to steady myself and then begin again. By the time I found my release, it consumed me, body, mind, and soul. It was the most intense pleasure I had ever had in my entire life. It was a good thing we were outside. I was not able to control my powers as I had this morning. The magic rippled off of my body and transformed the surrounding area. What had been a simple yet beautiful lakeshore with a pebble beach and soft surrounding grass now looked like the Garden of

Eden. Lush bushes full of flowers abounded, vines and moss in vivid greens clung to the trees, and wildflowers had taken the spot of almost every blade of grass surrounding us.

We lay on the ground, my head resting on Theo's chest, his fingers gently brushing and tickling my back. His other hand reached up and pressed tenderly under my chin to lift my head. He kissed me deeply and soundly once more before removing his hand and letting my chin fall to where it had been resting moments before.

As we laid content in our quiet companionship, I examined our surroundings a little more. I hadn't really thought about what time of year it was until now. I had spent more time with Theo and the pack than I had in any one place since leaving Chicago. Lying in this beautiful place made me realize we were in true summer now and the air was hot. A cool breeze from the lake played across our bare skin and made it quite comfortable to be outside naked. We stayed there, just lying in the sun with each other until it was early evening. Theo sighed and said we should head back. I didn't hide the disappointment on my face. Theo laughed lightly, kissed me on the cheek, and said, "Don't worry, our day isn't over yet."

He watched in awe once more as I changed into a wolf and we took off at a light run back to the house. We arrived where I had left my clothes just as the sun was setting. Being a werewolf, Theo could choose to change back into his human form with or without clothes. I was not so fortunate. He stood there watching me with glowing eyes as I slipped my jeans and t-shirt back on. "Come with me," he said, smiling. He took my hand and led me to the front lawn. Everyone in the pack must have left while we were away. No sounds of laughter or conversation drifted our direction as we headed toward the front of the main house. When we walked onto the lawn my breath caught in my chest. The lawn had been transformed. White Christmas lights decorated the area and there was a private table set for two, complete with glowing candles. Chilled wine and covered plates waited for us with a small note from Martha.

> *Enjoy, you two! The food should still be hot and*
> *don't worry about the pack, Sebastian and I*
> *have everything covered!*
>
> *~Martha*

I smiled at her thoughtfulness. Martha had such a good heart; I could feel it every time I looked at her. The smell of her homemade cooking had me salivating. Theo pulled my chair out for me and scooted me in after I'd sat.

"Would you like some wine?"

"Umm… I've never had any."

"Never?"

"No. I was still pretty young when everything started to go south for humans. I never really got the opportunity." Theo nodded and poured me a small glass.

The wine was bubbly and tickled my tongue. It was slightly tart but crisp and refreshing after our run home. I took a few small sips and set the glass back down, not wanting to drink too much too fast. Theo uncovered our plates and my stomach grumbled in anticipation. Before us lay stuffed chicken breasts dripping in what smelled like a mushroom sauce. Vegetables smothered with butter and cooked to perfection had me quickly helping myself. After several bites I noticed that Theo hadn't eaten even one. I finished chewing and set my fork down. Theo was chewing his bottom lip and his brow was slightly furrowed. "Aren't you hungry?" I asked.

"What? Oh, right, I am, umm… I want to make a toast." He seemed distracted as he reached for his glass and nearly knocked it over. His quick reflexes helped him to save the glass from tipping and he raised it quickly.

"To the new life you have been thrown into and accepted with grace and accomplishment." His compliment brought a shy smile to my face and I lifted my glass to meet his. While the sip I took was small, Theo downed nearly half his glass in one gulp. Setting it down, he quickly wiped his hands down his thighs. "Is the food all right?" he asked. I stated that it was delicious while noting he still hadn't taken a single bite. "Good… good." He wiped his hands across his thighs again.

"Theo, is everything all right?" Since arriving back at the house, he'd seemed tense and distracted.

"Andie, I…" He stood quickly, almost knocking his chair backwards, took a few paces away from the table, and walked back. Holding his hand out, he reached to help me stand. I was so nervous; we had had such a wonderful day together and now it seemed as if something were terribly wrong.

The few bites of food I had eaten felt like a giant rock weighing down my insides.

"Andie... do you like it here?"

"Of course I do." And I meant it – this was the first place I had felt at home since I was a child.

"Will you stay? Forever?"

"Theo?"

As we stood facing each other, Theo dropped to one knee. The world stopped. "Marry me, Cassandra. Be my wife. I will honor, love and protect you to no end, for as long as I live. Please, say you will stay here and spend the rest of your life with me."

I didn't breathe. I couldn't. The past months flashed through my mind. Sure, it had only been a short period of time, but I couldn't picture my future without him.

"Yes." My answer was hardly a whisper. I tried again, "Yes!" I said it louder this time and it felt real, spreading warmth across my stomach and into my chest. The answering smile that spread across Theo's face brought tears to my eyes and he jumped to his feet, sweeping me into a crushing hug. He spun me around and with the little breath I had I giggled.

He set me down and laced his fingers into my hair. "I love you." He said it with such tenderness that I thought my heart would burst from happiness. He brushed a light kiss across my lips before releasing me and reaching into his pocket. He pulled out a simple yet stunning ring, with a silver band and a small solitary diamond. "It's not as big as you deserve, but it was my mother's... I found it in my father's old things..."

That the memory brought him pain hurt me, but I felt honored to be wearing something of his mother's. "It's beautiful, and perfect." I smiled at him as he slipped the ring onto my finger. He swept me up in his arms once more and this time there was no light brush of skin, but a deep and all-consuming meeting of lips. I needed him, and he needed me. The homemade meal forgotten, Theo carried me inside. The rest of the night was spent wrapped in each other, making love and talking excitedly.

CHAPTER 20

OUR HAPPY RESPITE FROM REALITY DIDN'T LAST LONG. THE following morning our engagement was announced to the pack and was met with joy and well wishes. After a cheerful, late breakfast, I gave Theo a lingering hug and kiss goodbye before heading out to meet Anthea for more training. As I pulled away, Theo's fingertips brushed across the back of my arms and left goosebumps in their wake. "See you tonight." The gentle whisper was enough to make me squirm and rush out the door, knowing that the sooner I met with Anthea and trained, the sooner I could come back home to Theo. *Home.* I was truly home now. The thought only added to my joy and broadened the grin on my face.

When I came to the designated clearing where I would meet Anthea, I was surprised to also see Florence and Dorothy. Usually the three witches alternated working with me, each of them having their own knowledge and experience to add to my training. After seeing the ring on my finger, the three of them hugged me in congratulations and then the four of us sat in a circle. Together we performed some simple relaxation techniques and then I continued to practice as I had before at pushing the boundaries of my magic. Well into the afternoon I finally began to tire.

"Enough for today, child." Anthea's smooth voice brought me comfort. By now I had mastered my ability to make anything grow, or make the plants move at my will. I could control the weather, I could locate and connect with any living thing, be it plant or creature, anywhere in the world with some simple concentration. I could sense if someone were trying to be deceptive towards me, and I could sense at the deepest part of their being whether they were good or evil. Although the line between good and evil was so blurred sometimes it was more of a spectrum than a distinct "line" between the two. I could transform with the elements like the nymphs of old, turning my skin to match the earth, wind, water, and even, to my surprise, fire. The flames left a tickling sensation on my skin that was actually rather pleasant. I could even transform into other animals, not just a wolf, if I chose, though that was still more difficult than anything else I had already mastered.

Once more the three witches formed a circle sitting on the ground with me and we all joined hands. "I feel you have completed your training with us, child." Anthea squeezed my hand as she smiled at me with tears brimming her eyes.

"What? Why?" Although I had mastered so much, I enjoyed the presence of the witches, especially Anthea, and felt empowered by their support and guidance.

"You have learned all you will from us; what you have left to learn, you must do on your own." This time it was Florence who had spoken. "I would like to lead us all, in saying a prayer and asking for a blessing on whatever journey your life may take." I smiled and gave a small nod. "But first, Cassandra, I have a message for you," Florence continued. "One of our sisters is gifted with the occasional glance at what the future may hold. It is never a very clear picture, as the future can change based on what one may decide to do or not, but nonetheless, there is usually a lesson to be learned from her visions. She asked me to warn you. To tell you that your future holds both great joy and great sorrow. That the decisions you will have to make may cause you pain. Your purpose, your path, your destiny to balance the world, may force you to do things that you would otherwise never choose in a million years. But yours is a path guided by the holy mother, the bearer to us all, and so you must never forget your purpose: to bring balance and harmony to the world, even if it does not bring such gifts to yourself."

My heart had gone from racing to almost stopped at the message Florence delivered. It made little sense to me, but I could feel the importance of the words as the message was delivered. I nodded my head once more, this time much more solemn and serious. Florence gave a small sigh and a tight smile before proceeding with the prayer and blessing their entire coven wished to bestow upon me. With her final words, each of the witches embraced me tightly and whispered that they would be there to serve if ever I needed them before leaving.

As excited as I was that morning to get home, I took my time walking the now familiar path back to the house. The message Florence had delivered had my mind reeling. What kind of decision would I have to make that could cause so much joy and so much pain all at once? By the time I made it back to the house, I'd decided to put it out of my mind. No use worrying about it when I had no clue what it meant. Besides... without my training with the witches, I now had plenty of time to plan a wedding!

Theo had told me that any kind of wedding would make him happy, so long as I was the one at the end of the aisle with him, his only request being that the entire pack be invited to the ceremony. Martha happily agreed to help me with anything she could. Seating arrangements and food were my biggest problem, but Martha quickly told me not to worry. There were plenty of chairs and tables to accommodate everyone for both the ceremony and the party afterwards, and with so many willing hands to help, setup would not be an issue. As for the food, she asked me if I had any special requests. Not knowing what the pack, or even Theo, would like best, I told her whatever she felt like making was sure to be wonderful. She gave me a cheerful smile and patted me on the back of the hand. We set the date for one week after Theo's proposal. No one felt the need to wait any longer than was necessary. I would have even opted for sooner had Martha not insisted we wait at least a week. That night Martha asked to have a private word with Theo. Once in our room, I asked Theo about it. "Nothing you need to worry about," was all he answered with.

"You're hiding something. Even if it wasn't completely obvious, I can still sense it."

Theo chuckled and kissed me on the forehead. "Please set your beautiful mind to rest, my love. Martha simply asked for my help arranging a wedding gift for you."

"A gift? But she's already helping me so much! How could I accept more from her?"

"Mmmmm," was all the noise he made as he nuzzled the soft spot on my neck just below my ear. The gentle kisses he then trailed down my shoulder succeeded in distracting me. When the heat of his lips continued down to my collarbone, I leaned back, lying on the bed. Theo followed, continuing his travels to first my right nipple and then my left. The mixture of his warm mouth and the texture of the now slightly moist fabric of my shirt grating against my nipples had the now familiar desire pooling between my legs. The contrast of his rough hands gently pushing my loose t-shirt up made my skin start to burn. I quickly disposed of my own clothing, wanting to give him access to my whole body. The thought that it might be better for me to start sleeping naked quickly entered my mind before being pushed back out by the entrance of his fingers into my now slick apex. His probing fingers were gentle at first, but it wasn't what I wanted, not right now. Right now I wanted him to take me, to claim me as his. I voiced my desire aloud and a deep rumble echoed from Theo's chest as he pulled back from me and stood at the edge of the bed. Hooking his hands behind my bent knees, he pulled me closer so that my bottom was right at the edge of the bed, with my legs wrapped around him. His hands moved quickly from behind my knees, scooping around the back of my hips and grabbing my ass.

He thrust into me and I cried out in relief at the full feeling of him inside of me. Every time he thrust another shock of pleasure would consume me. My breathing was already ragged, my mind lost except to focus on the feeling of him sliding in and out. His left hand remained hooked around my hip while the thumb of his right hand found the sensitive nub just above where he'd entered. The combination of his thumb circling me there and the now deep and quick movements of his hips were enough to make my hands fist into the covers. My release came fast, causing me to scream his name and making all of my muscles contract hard around him. In my blissful state I barely registered him finding his own climax. Theo stilled for only a few moments, his chest heaving deep breaths, before he began to move inside me once more. This time was slower, but my sensitive skin delighted in the slow rubbing pressure. Changing his position slightly once more, he ran his hands down my legs until they found my ankles locked behind him. He skillfully unhooked them and slid each leg up one at a time until they were resting on his shoulders. Continuing his steady pulses, he began to lean forwards. The action caused me to curl into a ball with my head almost to my knees. The change allowed Theo to push even deeper. His face was barely out of reach for me to kiss, but the look he gave made me melt into him, made my whole body flood with heat. His eyes were glowing but there was no mistaking the combined look of primal need and passionate desire written on his face. Before he finished with me I had found my climax an additional three times. My body felt limp with satiated exhaustion. Curling onto our sides, Theo pulled me in close. He kissed my hair before whispering that he would never get enough of me and that he loved me. I had never dreamed of loving someone as much as I did him.

The following morning, I awoke to knocking on the bedroom door. Realizing that Theo was no longer in bed next to me, and that I was still completely naked, I asked whoever it was to wait a moment and quickly dresses. When I was finished I opened the door to find Sebastian waiting for me.

"I'm to escort you, Martha, and a few of the other women to the town."

To town? What for? I wondered.

"Martha sent me to wake you up. She has some breakfast waiting for you and wants to leave in about thirty minutes."

"I'll be right down," I assured him. The door quickly snapped shut. Despite his gruff exterior, I had gotten to know Sebastian much better since I first arrived, and now felt comforted rather than disturbed by his presence. Thirty minutes was enough for me to rinse quickly in the shower, brush the "sex-tangles" out of my hair, and hurry downstairs for some of the toast and eggs Martha had waiting. Despite my multiple inquires, she refused to tell me why we were going in to town, or where I might find Theo. Resigned to the fact that she meant to surprise me, we headed out.

I was indeed surprised when I found out how large our party was. Besides myself and Martha, there were two older women whom I recognized and had spoken with several times, as well as Emma, the petite girl who had brought me my clothes, food, and books when I stayed in the small guest cabin. Apart from us, there was also Sebastian and three other of the men who ran patrols around the territory. I had expected to have to walk to the town, but instead a large van pulled up around the front of the house. Our party, plus the driver, rounded our number out to ten. We all squeezed and squashed into the van and headed towards town.

Martha hadn't blindfolded me, but it didn't matter. Stuck between Sebastian and James, one of the guards, I could hardly see anything past their broad shoulders and chests. As a result, the look on my face was nothing but genuine surprise when I stepped out of the van in front of a bridal shop. Martha took my arm in hers.

"It may not have all the markings of a traditional wedding, but every bride deserves a beautiful gown to wear the day she takes her vows. And you'd better believe I grabbed Theo's measurements for a tux before we left," she added with a conspiratory wink.

We all headed to the abandoned bridal shop. James smashed a small hole in one of the glass doors so he could unlock them and let us all in. Two guards remained at the front of the shop, two were posted in back, and Sebastian was stationed inside with us.

"Theo was rather concerned with me taking you to town, what with all this business about his father and the vampires... but I wouldn't take no for an answer so he agreed only if we took 'protection' with us." She chuckled. "Protection... I'd wager you could take on any danger we met all on your own!"

"Now!" Martha exclaimed, "What kind of dress would you like? They are all marked at the very affordable price of free, and the lovely ladies who agreed to come with us are here to help you pick and try on as many as you would like. Us older gals are happy to alter anything, should you find something you like not in your size." I couldn't help it. I leapt toward Martha and enveloped her in a bear hug. Having no mother of my own, it meant the world to me that Martha had arranged this trip and accompanied me. My eyes filled with tears and Martha tisked at me. "Now, now, you're not supposed to cry until AFTER you find the dress!" I pulled away and gave an excited nod.

I spent the next several hours trying on dresses. All of the women there seemed to be enjoying themselves, helping me find a new dress, try it on, and give their opinion on the shape or style. Sebastian stood by, stoically not making any faces or rolling his eyes. At long last we found the one. It needed some very simple altering, just a few "tucks" here and there would make it a perfect fit. Even Sebastian gave an approving nod.

We quickly cleaned up the mess we had made; placing all of the unwanted dresses back onto the racks, and headed for the car. While trying to pile everyone in, I began to feel odd. Something was wrong. Sebastian must have noticed the change in my body language because he made a simple hand signal and the guards moved in unison. They pinned all of us between the half circle they formed and the van. All of them were crouched, ready to act if need be. As the moments ticked by, my feelings came into sharper focus. With a gentle hand and calm voice I whispered to Sebastian, "Sebastian, I don't think it's a threat. There is someone around the corner of that building over there. She's hiding and terrified. I can feel her, but I cannot see anything that would lead me to believe she means us harm… I think its Izzy."

Izzy… the only other time I had seen her was when she'd been running from and terrified of Sebastian. I could still picture her frightened wide eyes silently begging with me. The memory was all it took and I found her with my mind. I could hear her every thought and feel the crazed adrenaline coursing through her veins. She had been used by her Alpha as a scapegoat and then abandoned by her pack. She had been on the run alone since Roderick had freed her from the cell in the basement and then killed the guard himself to blame it on her. Her wolf was half crazy from the lack of a pack to link to. As gently as I could I reached out to her, spoke to her through the newly formed mental connection.

"*Izzy?*" I could feel her heart rate pick up, and her confusion at hearing a voice in her head, thinking she had finally gone mad. "*Izzy, everything is all right, it's Andie… the girl from the grocery store. Do you remember me?*"

"*What do you want? Where are you?*" She was panicked.

"*Izzy, please, we're not going to hurt you. Come back to the house with us. I'm going to send James over, he won't hurt you, he's only coming to help.*"

With quick and whispered words I told Sebastian what had happened. He huffed that I had sent James instead of him, but given his last encounter with Izzy I thought it better.

James came back with a wild-looking Izzy. Her hair was a knotted mess, her cheeks smudged with dirt. Her pupils were shining and you could see her wolf close to the surface, ready to run at any moment. She was shaking from head to toe. With Martha's help, the two of us were able to gently coax her into the van. Four of the six guards decided they would do a quick scout of the area and then follow behind in wolf form. Sebastian was one of the ones who stayed behind.

A few miles from the house, I reached out to Theo using my mental link and warned him we were bringing Izzy back with us. Theo met us in front of the house. He had asked everyone else to leave so he could greet Izzy alone. As fragile as her psyche was at the moment, having too many people around would not have been the best thing for her. When I saw him, I disapproved of the clear Alpha stance he had taken, but when Izzy saw him she responded instantly. I could feel her less dominant wolf begin to relax as it recognized Theo as an Alpha, someone who would protect her. Theo spoke to her briefly, assuring her that after learning of Roderick's betrayal and knowing that she had done nothing wrong, she would be welcomed by all back into the pack. Her whole body sagged with relief and tears filled her eyes once more. Theo asked Martha to take her to the kitchen and get her something to eat while he spoke to me in private for a few minutes. Martha readily agreed and placed a gentle arm around Izzy's waist to lead her inside.

"How was your trip?" The grin he suppressed let me know that he knew what I had been doing.

"It was wonderful! And I found the perfect dress."

"Oh? Tell me about it."

"Fat chance. Sorry babe, you are getting no hint of what it looks like until you see me in it the day of."

Theo's grin broke into a true smile. "It doesn't matter what the dress looks like. You will be stunning. You always are." My cheeks flushed and I kissed him. "I have another surprise, well two actually, and then when we are done, I wonder if you wouldn't mind helping with Izzy? Getting her set-tled back into her old room while she adjusts back to the pack? She seems pretty fragile right now, and I think you could help her tremendously."

I was all too happy to agree, seeing as I was about to suggest the same arrangement. But another surprise? "I'm beginning to like surprises," I teased. Theo took my hand and led me inside. Up the stairs we passed his room and walked to another door. It was a large oak French door and when he opened it, I was slightly confused. The room was mostly empty except for a large four-poster bed and a few dressers. There was also a small balcony and a large master bath and closet.

"It's the Alpha's room," Theo clarified. "I emptied it today while you were gone. Got rid of all of my father's stuff. I kept a few things; family pictures and a few of my mother's old things he still had in here, but I had them boxed and moved to one of the storage closets. I figured if I'm going to be Alpha it's about time I moved in here. However, it's going to be your room too, so I thought we could arrange and decorate it together. Make it our own." The simple gesture had me hugging him around the neck and kissing him once more. Theo responded with a deep growl and I could feel his growing affection pressing against me. He sighed deeply before pulling away. "Come on, or I'll never get to show you the other surprise."

This time he led me back outside. A short distance into the woods we came upon what looked like another one of the small cabins. The thought that I would never know where everything was in this complex briefly passed through my brain before realizing what Theo had done to the cabin. Based on my knowledge of the other small cabins surrounding the area, he had replaced all of the outer walls with glass doors that could be turned and left open or shut tight together. Either way, it allowed one to be outside in nature, while still being inside. The interior still had a small private bathroom, but he had added a skylight that could be opened if desired in there. The bed was given privacy by a heavy gauze curtain that wrapped around.

"It's our private getaway. I've been working on it with some of the other pack when you go to meet with the witches. It's also my wedding gift to you. This way, even when inside, you can still be surrounded by the outdoors."

"Theo... it's perfect!" Perfect was an understatement. I loved everything about the little cabin and what it would provide for us in the future. After a few quick minutes of exploring the inside, we headed back to the house. Izzy had already finished eating and Martha had her waiting for me in the kitchen with a glass of tea.

"Come on Izzy, let's get you cleaned up." I took her hand and followed her directions to her old bedroom. I turned the water to the shower on and stepped out so she could undress and shower. I left while she showered, assuring her through the bathroom door I would be right back with something clean to wear. The only problem was I was unsure where to find anything. After all my time here, I still only had a few sets of clothes, and I had simply had to ask either Theo or Emma and they had provided the clothes for me. I quickly reached out to Emma's mind and asked her. She responded by telling me to meet her in the hall by the kitchen. She showed me where the laundry room was for the main house as well as the large closet that was attached to it. Clothes of many sizes were stored there for any wolf that had been traveling through and in need of refuge before the world learned of the existence of werewolves. I grabbed a soft cotton nightgown, a pair of comfortable-looking jeans, and a simple t-shirt. Just before leaving I turned back around and after some searching found some clean underwear. There were a few unopened packages, the kind you used to buy from Walmart, in a drawer, then headed back to Izzy. She had just stepped out of the shower when I returned. Wrapped in a towel I could see that she was practically skin and bone and covered in bruises. I helped her dry off and change into the nightgown. Though it was still only late afternoon, she looked exhausted. I quickly stepped away once more to grab a hairbrush and returned to help Izzy brush her hair until it was dry. As I brushed we talked. With each bit of conversation, she relaxed. I told her about everything that had happened here at the house since I had seen her that first day in the store, and she told me about the horrors she faced being on her own, about her wolf almost becoming crazed and dangerous due to her lack of a stable pack, and about being constantly worried she would be found by either one of our patrols or by the vampires. I asked at one point why she had never left the territory. She shrugged and simply replied that she hadn't wanted to wander too far from the pack, even though she didn't think she would be welcomed back, it was her home, and she couldn't leave it.

Although I was bursting with more questions, I gave her a genuine hug and sent her under the covers. I'd never had any siblings, but I imagined this is what it would have felt like tucking one of them in at night. Izzy was asleep before I closed the door.

That night Theo and I went to the little cabin he had renovated for me. The nights were still warm enough that we opened every glass panel on the walls. It was like sleeping outside, except we still had the luxury of a comfy bed.

Over the next week, my time was spent only a few ways. Most mornings I spent with Martha going over wedding plans, although I now had the help of about half a dozen women in the pack who helped us plan. I didn't mind the extra help – not only did it give me the opportunity to get to know some of the pack better, but they all respected my wishes about the day and I knew with their help it would be the perfect wedding. I even included Izzy in some of the planning, and she began to break out of her shell a bit and rejoin the community of wolves we lived in. The afternoons were spent mostly with Izzy, either walking through the woods and talking or simply doing chores around the house. Emma would sometimes join us and I could tell that, where there hadn't been much of a friendship there before between the two young women, there was one growing now. I would notice them often chatting and laughing around the house. The evenings were spent with Theo, decorating and arranging our new room to our liking. With Martha's help I surprised him one evening with a group of pictures for one of the walls. I had recruited several of the pack members to try and sneak candid shots of the two of us together and a few of them had turned out quite impressive. Our nights were filled with love and passion, and on more than one occasion we found ourselves in a post-coital cuddle, gazing at the stars in comfortable companionship in the little glass cabin until the sun began to rise.

CHAPTER 21

THE DAY BEFORE THE WEDDING FOUND ME WITH NOTHING TO do. Sebastian had taken Theo out for what he called a "bachelor party." It included a group of a dozen of the men, ranging in ages from sixteen to mid-forties, that went out for a day-long run and hunting expedition. All of the wedding plans were set for the following day, and even Izzy and Emma had made plans to have a girls-day-in with movies and junk food. They had invited me, but being cooped up inside had not been appealing. Instead I had wandered to the glass cabin and was sitting with all of the doors wide open, reading a book I had found in the entertainment room at the house. The plot was not very captivating and my mind kept wandering. After about an hour of trying to force myself to read I gave up and decided instead to work on my magic. I hadn't really practiced anything since my last meeting with the witches. I sat calmly and did some breathing exercises to clear my mind. Thinking of Theo, I decided to try and explore the territory with my mind, reach out to every creature within its boundaries.

I knew Theo so well now it was not at all difficult to find him, to feel the joy he had leading the group he was running with as they hunted down a large buck. I enjoyed connecting with him for a few minutes before leaving him to his fun. I started on the east side of the territory and worked my way west, feeling the life that filled the area. Then something odd happened. As I traveled through the woods in my mind's eye, it became foggy. There was no animal life to be found in the area, and the life of the plants, that I could usually detect so well, came to me in a sluggish hazy form. It made my body turn cold. My breathing became shallow and labored. I knew I should stop, to withdraw my mind from the outside world, but I felt compelled to continue, to try and find the cause. I managed to reach out of the darkness in time to call for Martha to help me before passing out.

"Where is she!?" I could hear Theo crash through the front doors of the house before his feet pounded up the stairs to our room. I had already reached out to him, to tell him I was fine, but he wouldn't believe it, not until he saw me with his own eyes. When Martha had found me, she said I was cold to the touch and so pale it was if the life had been drained out of me. By the time she had me moved back to the main house, I was coming to, and was now sitting in one of the two overstuffed armchairs in our room, wrapped in a blanket and being forced to drink hot tea. I felt perfectly fine, and slightly irritated that Theo would not listen to my mental plea to continue his hunt and not come home. He was the biggest worrier, but despite my annoyance at his overbearing concern, I knew his worry came from a place of love.

Sagging with relief when he saw me, he kissed me deeply and asked if I was sure that I felt OK.

"I'm fine… but… well, you're not going to like it, but I'd like to try what I was doing again."

Theo looked at me as if I had lost my mind. "Are you crazy? It sounds like whatever you were doing nearly killed you! Martha said you looked pale as death!"

"That's just it! Death!"

"What?!"

"Theo, listen. All this time, when I reach out with my mind, when I explore, a part of me always keeps trying to track and locate the vampires. I've never been able to do it because I can only focus on life, and they are not living. But today, I think I may have stumbled upon them by accident. If I'm looking for them, I can't look for life, I have to look for the absence of it. Get it?"

Theo looked slightly confused, but after a few more minutes of talking him into it, the prospect of me possibly finding the vampires won over his concern. The only condition being that if I began to feel as I had before in the cabin, I would stop immediately.

When I reached out this time, I expanded the view I saw in my head. I didn't focus on one living thing at a time, but rather the entirety of our territory as well as those surrounding us. This time I could see it: it was as if there were blank spots on the map, areas of darkness where it was hard to see. I could focus on the plants, but even they were hard to find. The cold feeling of death was pressing in on me. I could hear Theo calling my name so I stopped. His beautiful face marred with lines of worry was the first thing that swam into my line of vision. I smiled and placed a hand on his cheek, and he in turn sighed and leaned into my palm.

"Theo, it's them."

"You're sure?"

"Yes, I don't know if your father is with them. I still can't find him thanks to that witch's magic, but it's the vampires for sure. And it's not good. You need to call a pack meeting." The grave expression on Theo's face had my heart breaking. I wanted to hold him, to shut out the world that kept trying to come between us. But it simply would not do. I settled for a quick kiss before telling him everything so that we could present it to the pack as a team.

An hour later the entire pack had managed to cram into the council room and the hall just outside. Theo quickly quieted them. "As you all know by now, our former Alpha, my father, Roderick, betrayed this pack. He became worried someone would take the Alpha position from him and to prevent it from happening he went so far as to murder two of our own and sell information on our pack to our enemies, in exchange for assurance of maintaining his status. Since his betrayal was brought to light, he has fled, we think to side with the vampires, his goal to eventually take the pack back as his own." There were some cries of outrage at this statement. "I will not let him do that. I am your Alpha now. And like a true Alpha, I would give my life for the safety of this pack." This time it was cries of support that rang quickly through the crowd. "You all know by now that Cassandra, the incredible woman who has agreed to marry me, is no ordinary woman. She is the daughter of Mother Earth, sent here to help balance the good and evil on Earth. As I'm sure you have also noticed, she has the amazing ability to connect with any one of us, at any given time. Thanks to her powers, we have discovered something extremely unsettling. The vampires are coming for us. We know that they want Cassandra, they know what she is. We can only assume they know this thanks to Roderick, but there is nothing to be done about that now. They are coming, soon. Andie has been able to detect them along the borders of our territory, and not just one coven either. There seems to be a large number of them gathering at several locations surrounding our territory. It appears they are planning to try and invade, to take our territory by force. You were all planning on coming to the wedding tomorrow, but I must ask you to come here now, as soon as you can. The entire pack will stay at the central compound until it is deemed safe to return to your own homes. I myself will lead a recon team to try and gather information about when the vampires will attack." At some point during his speech I had grabbed his hand. I stood next to him, filled with pride at the love and care he had for his pack. For our pack. He ended the meeting and everyone quickly dispersed to gather their things and settle in. The main house could provide rooms for many but not all. Others that lived in the immediate complex opened their homes to anyone needing an extra bed or couch to sleep on. I tried to convince Theo that I needed to join the recon team but he would not hear it. Instead he set me to the task of helping everyone get organized and settled in.

By the time Theo and the rest of the team returned, it was almost two in the morning. A few others and myself were still awake and waiting in the kitchen. My nerves were frayed; I had been keeping up with each one of them the whole time they were gone, worried that they might get caught. Luckily, everyone was returning safely. The mood in the room when they entered, however, was anything but cheerful.

Theo sank down into a chair and ran his hands through his hair in frustration. Martha and I quickly heated some leftovers we had saved from dinner for the recon party. While the rest of the team seemed thankful for the food, neither Theo nor Sebastian touched a single bite. I sat beside Theo and grabbed his hand in mine. "Tell me."

Theo gave a great sigh and answered. "They are swarming our borders. Gathering their numbers before launching a massive attack. Roderick is there, giving them information about our numbers, the layout of the land, and everything he thinks he knows about you. There must be close to a thousand of them already, hiding in the buildings in the old towns. Some have even camped out with tents that block out the sun. We caught wind that the attack isn't for another two nights. I can only imagine it is to wait for more of them to show up, otherwise why would they risk waiting and being so close?" The worry and stress Theo felt was etched into every line of his face, the set of his shoulders. I wished I knew how to help…

Help. I could help!

"Theo!" He looked shocked at my excited tone. "Theo, listen! How many other wolf packs are within a day's running distance from here?"

"I don't know… five, maybe six?"

"And how many witch covens?"

"I have no idea, three that I know of. But Andie, I don't see what this has to do with…"

"We call for help. We reach out to our allies and grow our own numbers."

"Andie, we're not exactly allies with those other wolves, and especially not the witches. Besides, we have no way of getting ahold of them all so quickly."

"I do." Theo's eyes lit with understanding. "And they will come, if I ask them to. If their surAvani calls on them, they will answer." It made me nervous to say it. I was a little unsure, but it was worth the try.

Shortly after dawn, I finally stopped trying to reach out to the other packs and covens. My body was completely drained and it felt as if my mind was mush, but I had used my powers to reach out to every living creature in the area. I had contacted over three hundred wolves, around fifty witches, and even a small group of humans I found camping in the nearby area. The humans I had warned to move on and quickly, but the rest had been informed of who I was and that we needed help. Shock was the general first impression everyone had after I initiated contact. But by the end of the speech I had perfected after about the twentieth time I had repeated it, it seemed as if all of them would come. It turned out most of the wolves were ready for a war with the vampires, and the witching covens would not refuse a request from the surAvani.

"OK you two… get a few hours rest and then we have a wedding to put on!" Martha had just walked in to start making her morning cup of coffee when she saw me and Theo still sitting at the table. Sebastian was there as well, although his face was buried in his arms and we'd heard soft snoring coming from his direction for the last hour or so. Theo and I glanced at each other before addressing Martha.

"Martha, I don't think with everything else going on…"

"Maybe it would be better if we postponed…"

"Nonsense. You love each other. As far as we know we still have one more night before the vampires attack, and who knows what could happen after that. Life is short, I learned that the hard way when my Michael left this world. So, this wedding will continue as planned, just with the addition of some new guests."

There was no point in arguing with her. Theo punched Sebastian in the shoulder, causing him to snort and jerk awake. "Bas… I need you to organize the scouts. Triple the patrol, but make the coverage zone smaller. It's only to include the few square miles where everyone is staying. After that I need you to take a nap. I can't have my best man falling asleep standing behind me at the altar." With a groggy smile Sebastian agreed and headed off to do as Theo asked. "And as for you…" He kissed my forehead, my nose, and then finally my lips. "I'll see you this afternoon. I'll get ready in my old room so you can have the Alpha suite." With a quick nod to Martha, he headed out the door.

"Come on dear, you need a few hours sleep before we get you ready." The motherly way she shooed me up the stairs to the bedroom had me smiling. If I could not have my own mother at my wedding, Martha was certainly an excellent substitute.

What seemed like only seconds after I had closed my eyes, Martha and Emma were waking me back up again. My body still felt tired, but my mind no longer felt like a cold bowl of oatmeal. My stomach did an odd fluttering at the thought that in a few hours, despite everything that was happening, I would be Theo's wife. Over the next two hours, I physically prepared myself to walk down the aisle. Mentally, I had a hard time focusing on anything except the upcoming battle. For it would be a battle, of that I had no doubt. My stomach fluttered again at my anxious thoughts. I showered, shaved, washed and dried my hair on my own. Then, thanks to the help of Martha, Emma, and Izzy, my hair was expertly curled, my nails painted, and my makeup applied flawlessly. My hair was pinned into a low updo, and I used my abilities to grow some white lilies to add in amongst the curls. My makeup was light and natural looking while bringing just a hint of color to my cheeks and lips. As harsh as I had been in the past about my looks, even I had to admit that I looked, and felt, pretty. Martha made me eat, saying that once I had the dress on and the ceremony started, I would forget about food, so I had better eat now. I nibbled on a sandwich and sipped some coffee but it all sat heavy in my stomach and made me nauseous. I finished what I could before telling Martha I couldn't eat anything else. She took everything away but placed a glass of ice water in front of me, and I did manage to drink all of that.

There was a sudden knock on the door. Emma and Izzy giggled and Martha hushed them before heading to the door and cracking it open. One glance and she opened the door farther to reveal Sebastian waiting on the other side. He still looked tired, but handsome in his formal attire.

"May I enter?"

"Of course, Sebastian."

"I was sent as the messenger. Apparently it's my duty as the best man to inform you that everything is set downstairs. We do have a schedule to keep because of obvious security concerns..." At this point Martha cleared her throat loudly. "...however, I have been informed that a bride is never late to her own wedding, everyone else is simply early. So whenever you are ready, I will be waiting just outside the door to escort you down to the front lawn." He bowed quickly and exited. Martha stared at him, her hands on her hips and shaking her head as he shut the door behind him. All that was left for me to do was dress. It didn't take long; the dress didn't have a lot of "fluff" to it. The simple satin gown had a high neck, with a small keyhole to show off the tiniest hint of cleavage. The straps were thin and led to an open back filled with lace. A small train completed the gown. It was not flashy, but it complemented every one of my small curves while still being elegant. I felt like a 40s movie star walking down the red carpet. I stayed barefoot, something I had decided so that as I walked down the aisle, I could leave flowers growing where my footprints would have been, like the first day I went outside after my nature ceremony. Martha embraced me, crying already, and told me I made a lovely bride. I returned the hug, and whispered a sincere thank you into her ear. She kissed me once on the cheek. "Come on, I suppose we had better not keep Theo waiting any longer." I nodded my agreement and took a deep breath to steady my all-too-active stomach. Sebastian, as promised, was waiting outside the bedroom door. He smiled and offered me his arm. Martha grabbed my hand and squeezed it once more before she and the other two girls made their way downstairs to find their seats.

CHAPTER 22

Sebastian and I made our way down the stairs and to the front door in silence. Before heading out ahead of me he turned to face me.

"Once I'm in place next to Theo, the music will start and then it's all you." He made an odd face before embracing me awkwardly. "Welcome to the family, sis. Do me a favor… take care of him, OK?"

"I will." It was all I could answer with before feeling myself begin to get choked up. Sebastian released me, straightened his jacket, and headed out the door. A few minutes later I heard the music begin to play. Theo was a big music fan, and amongst his vast music collection I managed to find an instrumental version of an old Beatles song. The slow beautiful melody was perfect for my walk down the aisle.

My first glimpse of outside was a little overwhelming. There were so many people! The members of the pack I was about to officially join, as well as several other new faces. I could only assume that they were early arrivals from other packs, come to help fight the vampires. The decorations were perfect, simple and minimal. White folding chairs filled either side of the aisle, and at the end, a trellis made of small wood branches wrapped with white Christmas lights donned the place we would say our vows. When my eyes finally met Theo's, I had to tell myself not to run down the aisle to him. Standing in his suit and tie, he was the perfection of male beauty, but his face was the only thing I focused on as I completed my journey to his side.

As there were really no more laws in place governing marriage, we had one of the older, well-respected members of the pack lead the ceremony. He spoke a few words about love and commitment before Theo and I spoke our own vows. Later, I wouldn't be able to recall exactly what had been said. I would only remember looking at him. I would remember thinking how happy I was, and the feeling of love and joy as it spread between us. We kissed and the crowd erupted in cheers.

The reception was subdued due to the general feeling of apprehension, but Theo and I didn't mind. It made it that much easier for us to excuse ourselves at the end of the meal and head towards the glass cabin. It had quickly become our favorite spot. At some point during the day, Theo, or someone directed by Theo, had come out to the cabin and hung more Christmas lights inside the cabin, and the doors were already standing open. The night was turning slightly cool, but it didn't matter. The heat of our passion kept us warm.

Theo peeled me out of the dress, the cool evening air and his hungry gaze giving me goosebumps. The clingy satin material and the lace back hadn't allowed me to wear much in the way of undergarments, so all I had underneath was a pair of pale pink underwear. Theo grabbed me and tossed me onto the bed. He quickly dispersed of his own clothing, leaving everything lying on the ground. He hastily found the seams in the underwear and ripped them apart. His heavy breathing matched my own as he took a long and sweeping gaze down my body. His fingertips trailed lightly from my collarbone to the edge of the small curls I had between my legs and back, causing my stomach to dip and clench in excitement.

"You are beautiful, and you are mine, my *wife,* my *mate.*" He kissed me and I ran my fingers into his hair, pulling him deeper into the kiss. His chest rumbled and he positioned himself between my legs before entering me. My body responded quickly to his, as it always did, and before long the moisture he had created between my legs made it easy for him to plunge deep and hard into me. My back arched with every thrust and Theo took advantage of my breasts being closer to his mouth. He suckled and gently nipped at the sensitive flesh that formed my hardened nipples. When he pulled away from me, I was momentarily confused. Theo grabbed my hips and flipped me over, then gently pulled me up until I was on all fours on the bed. He placed a knee between my legs, inching them a little farther apart before he entered me again from behind. One hand reached around my waist and began to play with the sensitive nub between my lower lips while the other hand ran the length of my back before reaching around to once again pay tribute to my breasts. I braced myself with my hands, needing every bit of him and meeting his every thrust forward with a small thrust of my own backwards. The hand playing with my breast left and traveled to my hip, giving him even more leverage. The motion of his fingers circling my swollen clitoris and the exquisite feeling every thrust brought me, meant it wasn't long before I found my release. My hands fisted in the covers and my head flung back as Theo quickened his pace for me. The pleasure ripped through me, pulsing through my body from my core to my fingertips and toes. But Theo was not done with me; he would tease and tug, rub, lick, and impale me until I had come three times before he finally allowed himself to find his own release.

Sweating and trying desperately to control our breathing, we lay, wrapped together and legs tangled until we finally drifted into sleep.

The following morning we woke early – a sense of foreboding filled the air. Martha had been right and I had forgotten about eating yesterday and I was starving, but I did not want to leave our little sanctuary. I knew as soon as we did the reality of what was to happen that night would set in. We would be pulled apart, taking on our respective duties to prepare everyone for what would happen once the sun set. As Theo made to get up, I reached out, stopping him by simply laying my hand on his chest. I raised myself up so I was closer to his eye level. I moved my hand from his chest to scrape my fingers across the stubble that had formed on his jaw. The look he gave me both melted and broke me.

"Andie, tonight..."

"Shhh. I don't want to talk about it." I crawled on top of him so we were face-to-face and pulled his lips to mine. There was no frenzied passion this time. It was the slow need of two people trying desperately to become one, before facing the uncertain future. We finally admitted we could no longer ignore reality and stood to dress before walking slowly, hand in hand, back to the main house.

CHAPTER 23

WHEN WE ARRIVED AT THE MAIN LAWN IT WAS PACKED. THE tension running through the crowd was hard to handle at first. Everyone's inner wolves were on edge from the onslaught of new scents. Add on top of that the apprehension of what was going to happen when we finally faced the vampires. Theo squeezed my hand and addressed me. "Do you think you could pinpoint who the Alphas are and ask them to join us in the council room?"

"Sure, should I ask the witches too?"

"Yes, but only their leaders as well."

I nodded quickly before closing my eyes and doing as he asked. It didn't take me long, so after a few minutes I opened my eyes again and Theo and I began to walk towards the council room. Sebastian was standing at the front door to the house, taking report from one of the patrols. When he finished, Theo asked him to join us as well.

Before long, those we had invited to join us arrived and we closed the doors. Including Theo and Sebastian, all seven of the Alphas, their Betas, and five witches, each the leader of their own coven, stood in the room. Adding all of our forces together we had a little over four hundred wolves, close to seventy witches, and me. The witches I had contacted initially had reached out to others they knew and many of them had shown up as well. As grateful as I was for the help that had come flooding in so fast, we were still outnumbered more than two to one. The witches would be important because they could handle more than one vampire at a time, but we also knew that the vampires would have some witches on their side as well.

"I want to thank you all for being here." Theo quickly addressed the group, who were all standing in a large circle. "You left your families and the safety of your home to stand and fight with us. It is a debt I will never be able to repay. I know that we all have our differences, but right now we face a common enemy. One that must be stopped, before they destroy us all." Many of the leaders nodded their agreement.

"We are still greatly outnumbered. Which is why I've called you all in here to discuss strategy. "

"We should attack now, while it's still daylight. It gives us the best advantage."

One of the other alphas interjected. Another responded to his statement.

"What good would that do? They're all hiding in old buildings. We would have to split up to attack each building, and we would have to go inside where there is no light to fight. This wouldn't give us an advantage, it would be giving them one." The alpha who spoke originally growled, as he did several of the wolves in the room crouched and started staring each other down.

"Stop it!" My scream caught everyone's attention and the growling that had filled the room a moment ago stopped. "Theo's right. We have an army of vampires waiting out there. It doesn't do us any good to fight amongst each other. Right now, you need to put your egos aside and work together to create a plan. Otherwise we're all dead." A few of them had the decency to hang their head in shame. I nodded to Theo who began the discussion again.

An hour later, we had a plan. We would wait for them to attack us. At least being out in the open would make it easier for the witches and me to see everything that was going on, and we could keep our numbers together. While we would fight as one, it was agreed that each pack leader would remain in control of their own packs, like Generals on the battle-field. It would be my job, since I could communicate at a distance with everyone, to coordinate the attacks. Theo also insisted that any children and any elders that were not fit to fight would be kept in our basement.

Since this was our home, we were the only group who had any children or elderly. The other leaders, agreed without question, and I was grateful that the children I had seen so long ago, playing tag out on the lawn my first day here, would not witness the fighting.

When we left the council room, several of the individuals who had been inside stopped shortly after entering the hall. Theo and I made our way through the small crowd and immediately knew why everyone was staring. Three humans stood near the entrance to the main house. Two men and a woman, all of whom appeared to be in their late twenties or early thirties. And all three were very fit.

"We're looking for Andie." The statement came from the bigger of the two males.

"I'm Andie," I answered.

The man who had spoken grinned broadly and stuck out his hand. "I'm John. This is Ryan and Marie. We were camped about a dozen miles out with two others when we got your message about leaving. The other two we were traveling with, they packed up, couldn't leave fast enough. But we're here to fight." A look of doubt crossed my face, and John saw it. "I know we're human. I know we don't have supernatural speed or strength; but we can fight, we want to fight. Even if between the three of us we only take down one vamp, that's still one less vampire in the world. We're willing to take that risk." I looked at Theo and he raised his eyebrows and shrugged. Sticking his own hand out, Theo shook hands with all three of them and introduced himself. Theo agreed to let the three humans fight alongside his own pack, but made it clear that if any of them changed their minds, we wouldn't think any less of them. After pointing them in the general direction of our pack, the three of them headed off.

The rest of the day was spent in what felt like a suspended reality. There were so many of us there, all waiting, and all saying what we hoped wouldn't be final goodbyes. Shortly before the sun began to set, everyone started to move into place. We would face them on the main lawn; we wanted to be able to see them coming. My heart had already started to race and my stomach had butterflies once more. I grabbed Theo and pulled him to me. He bent slightly so that we stood facing each other with our foreheads pressed together.

"I love you more than my own life." Theo whispered the words to me.

I held him tighter and whispered back, "I love you too," as I fought the tears that threatened to spill. With a deep breath, and a hard, long kiss to the man I loved, I turned to face the wooded area across from us. The sun was low on the horizon; only a small sliver of it remained. "They're coming." I could sense them, filling the woods usually so full of life with their deathly void. "*Get ready.*" I sent the message out mentally to everyone on our side. When the last rays of sunlight faded, the battle began.

CHAPTER 24

THERE WAS A MOMENT'S PAUSE WHILE EVERYONE SEEMED TO hold their breath, then the line crashed through the trees. Every movement turned into a blur as werewolves and vampires alike ran at full speed towards one another. Already the sound of battle screams and cries of pain filled my ears. I took a final deep breath and let my mind expand. I was linked with the mind of every werewolf and witch on the field, a mental part of every individual quarrel. The witches on our end took action, using their magic to throw vampires hundreds of feet in the air before they were ripped apart, only to be turned to ash carried away by the wind. Other witches were casting spells, ones that slowed the vampires down to human like speed. Struggling to move at a normal pace let alone the extremely excelled pace they were used to, it gave the wolves precious extra seconds to gain advantages. For a few moments my level of hope rose, but then the witches for the opposing side showed up. Suddenly wolves were dropping to the ground, screaming in agony as they began to bleed from every orifice on their bodies.

"*Distract them!*" I called mentally to our witches. They knew exactly what I meant, and soon the vampires and werewolves were left to battle it out as the witches engaged in their own duel. Sparks of magic flew through the air, lighting the battle that raged around me. More vampires continued to flood onto the field. I found Theo – he was close to Sebastian, the two brothers fighting together and already covered in ash. We were so outnumbered there was no reprieve. For every vampire that fell we were loosing two wolves. At this rate we wouldn't last long. I glanced at the tree line, still full of the pale, strong bodies rushing through the tree limbs…

The tree limbs. I could control the tree limbs. The words Theo once spoke to me sprang to the front of my mind. *"Listen to me carefully, Cassandra, because there may come a time when you need to know this. There are only a few ways to kill a vampire. Stake them in the heart with wood, burn them with sunlight or decapitate them."* I didn't stop to think. I focused on the woods and willed them to bend and twist at my command. The result was instantaneous. The tree branches sprang to life, wrapping around and trapping the vampires while still more branches moved and impaled, stabbing the vampires through their chests. A wooden stake through the heart… turned out a wooden branch worked just as well.

The harder it became for the vampires to get through the trees without being stabbed through the heart, the harder they fought to get through. I felt strong, could feel the energy of the Earth rising up, entering me wherever my feet touched the ground and flowing through my veins like a raging river. It felt as if nothing could stop me. The vampires changed tactics, trying to jump above the trees to get to the fight, but it didn't work. My branches flew up to meet them. The ones I didn't catch put up a fair fight against the wolves. Something strange was nagging me, but I couldn't figure out what it was. The battle was hard and both sides were showing the casualties to prove it, but the weight filling my chest had no explanation. My stomach started to flutter again and I pressed harder, pushing my powers to their limits.

I took some of my focus off the trees to do a mental check of everyone, and felt a stab at the realization that we had lost several of the witches, Anthea included. She had been such an important part of my transformation, and it felt as if a small chunk of my heart had been chipped away. Part of the nagging sensation now made sense… it seemed as if the vampires were not coming for me at all, they were trying their best to kill off the witches. What we'd thought would be a battle to try and dispose of me had turned into a witch-hunt, with the wolves doing their best to protect the witches. Few of them remained and as a result, the witches on the opposing side were now attacking the wolves as well. This couldn't be happening. We were fighting so well, how were we losing so many? I reached out to Theo, feeling his body raging, every ounce of energy he had being pushed into the fight he was a part of. But he was alive. I could survive anything as long as he was still with me. I pushed my focus back to the trees, trying desperately to kill as many vampires as I could.

Suddenly the world around me seemed to slow down. I was watching everything like parts from a movie played in slow motion before me. The remaining witches fighting for the vampires burst through the trees. There were not many of them and the pride I felt for the witches we had made as allies swelled in my chest. The vampires around them formed a wall, protecting the witches on their side as best they could. A giant bolt of magic flew through the air, hitting the spot where Sebastian and Theo stood fighting back to back. Why would the witches attack them? Sebastian went flying, landing several yards away, unmoving, but Theo remained. Abruptly, the slow motion scenes froze. Nothing moved, nothing happened. I was pulled from my body to a place I could only describe as 'somewhere else', the 'spirit world', a place neither here nor there where magic still ruled. I floated, looking at the frozen frame of time that encapsulated the battle raging around my body. My mind was then pulled away and I saw visions of the future playing, while Florence's warning echoed in my head.

"She asked me to warn you. To tell you that your future holds both great joy and great sorrow. That the decisions you will have to make may cause you pain. Your purpose, your path, your destiny to balance the world, may force you to do things that you would otherwise never choose in a million years. But yours is a path guided by the holy mother, the bearer to us all, and so you must never forget your purpose, to bring balance and harmony to the world, even if it does not bring such gifts to yourself."

In one vision, the spell that bound Theo released. I let go of my focus on the trees and refocused it in an effort to save him. Save him I did, and the battle was won, but it would be at the cost of my own life, and the unborn twins I had growing inside of me. As a confirmation of their existence, my stomach began to flutter once more, the butterflies that had been dancing in my belly over the last few days. At the end of the battle, the balance of good and evil would be unchanged because I would not be there to help the Earth heal itself.

In the other version of the future, Theo died, crushed slowly by the magical weight of the spell that held him. I listened to his agonized screams as my rage broke the last few remaining bonds to my human side that had limited my power. With those bonds broken, magic pulsed in visible waves from my body, eliminating all those who threatened to bring evil and darkness into the world. The remaining vampires and witches would be obliterated, but it would be too late to save the man I loved.

Thrust back into reality, I found myself sobbing, my chest feeling as though it would break in two. The vampires' tactic now made sense: they meant to distract me by attacking Theo, and therefore gain easier access to me. But their plan had failed. I knew the decision I had to make, the future I would have to choose. I looked at Theo through the ash-filled air and the dim light from all of the magic surrounding us and met his eyes. I reached out to him, showing him the possibilities the future held. Joy and sadness filled his face and I could see the tears filling his eyes as he nodded. The silent and last "I love you" that passed between us broke my heart in two and shattered any magical restraints I had left. As Theo died, right there before my eyes, my powers consumed me. They consumed everything. The blast of light that exploded from my body out across the field finished everything. As the light touched each vampire and each witch opposing us, they simply seemed to burn away, leaving nothing in their wake.

CHAPTER 25

THERE WERE NO MORE VAMPIRES TO FIGHT. NO MORE EVIL witches. The field filled with cheers as our side realized what had happened, but I couldn't hear them. I couldn't hear or feel the joy of the victory. As I knelt before the broken body of the man I loved, the man I had been privileged to call my husband for only one day, knowing that he was too far gone for even me to save, my world crumbled. The cry of pain and anguish that escaped my throat was enough to silence the crowd around me. I rocked back and forth on my knees, clutching my chest, trying to pull back together my broken heart, but it was no use. I clung to him, hoping that I would wake from this nightmare and find myself back in his arms, back in our glass cabin. Gentle but strong hands pulled me from the ground. I fought back, but I was too weak. The fight, the last wave of power that had ended the battle, and the loss of the person I loved more than anything, had drained me of everything I had. Sebastian pulled me to him, holding my body together as my soul tore into two. Eventually, either from the emotional pain or the physical weakness, I slipped into unconsciousness.

The next day, I woke to find myself lying in the bed in the Alpha's suite. The bed was too empty and too cold without Theo there to help fill it. I climbed from the bed, my body feeling numb. Silent tears made their way down my cheeks as I stepped into the bathroom. A quick glance in the mirror told me I was still covered in ash from the previous night. I barely felt the hot water as it cascaded down my skin. Even the tickling sensation that running water brought to my skin, hardly registered. I left the shower, still feeling numb and cold. I found some clothes, putting on a pair of plain jeans that belonged to me and a shirt that had belonged to Theo. It still smelled of him and the scent brought fresh tears to my eyes. I made my way slowly down the stairs and out onto the main lawn. The land looked awful. The grass had all been torn to pieces, the front row of trees stood with broken branches dangling from them, and the smell of burnt ashes still clung to the air.

Sebastian found me standing on the front porch looking over the now decimated lawn. He pulled me into a hug and whispered how sorry he was. To hear the strong and powerful man I now considered my brother say those words, while his voice cracked and tears sprang from his own eyes, nearly tore me in two all over again. He told me there would be a funeral at sunset for all those who'd died in the fighting. I nodded my understanding and pulled away from him. I wandered, not paying any attention to where I was going, until I found myself at the glass cabin. The vibrant vines and plants I had decorated it with still remained, but their colors seemed dull and ugly. I entered the cabin and found the bed. Crawling under the covers, I let my grief take hold of me once more and I cried until I had no more tears to shed. I lay there until the afternoon sun began to fade and then made my way to the small cemetery.

Members of all of the packs were there, as were several of the witches, and John, the only of the three humans to survive the battle, to pay their respects to those who had fallen. Everyone had suffered loss, and our sorrow banded us together. With the help of the remaining witches and myself, graves and headstones were quickly fashioned for every loved one who was no longer with us. Long after the others had made their way back to the main house, I lay on the ground next to Theo's grave.

As my fingers traced his name carved into the stone, my stomach began to flutter once more. It would be months before I would allow myself to feel joy again, but the twins I could feel growing inside of me every day made that possible. It would be years before my heart slowly began to feel whole again, and never would I love as I had loved Theo.

END

EPILOGUE

I SAT ON THE LAWN, ENJOYING WHAT LITTLE TIME I HAD watching the twins play with each other. The little girl, Emily, was much like me. Her dark curls bounced as she ran and played. She had inherited my gifts. She could make plants grow as she pleased, and could transform, to blend in with nature, or shape shift into an animal. So far she had only mastered the wolf form, but I had begun to work on the shape of an otter with her, on the occasions I was home.

The boy however, had taken after his father in both name and appearance. Little Theo, with his sandy untamable hair and hazel eyes, looked the carbon copy of the man I had loved and lost. While both my children were gifted, Theo was a mystery. Emily had power over nature just like me, but Theo had power over time. It didn't happen until he had turned three. He skipped forward in time. He was missing for a whole two hours before Martha had found him again, sitting in his room, playing with his toys. He had no idea he had even been gone.

It had been difficult for him to learn how to control, and I worried about what he was meant to do with his power. For now though, the sight of my children, their presence in my life, worked every day to mend the still broken shatters of my heart. I loved them, and spent any moment I could with them. I called them to me, and wrapped them in my arms. Tomorrow I would leave again, I would continue my search for evil in the world, and work as I had been destined to right the balance of good an evil.

Thank you so much for reading! I hope you enjoyed following Andie as she made her transition from human to surAvani. If you enjoyed what you read, please recommend this book to your friends, and keep a look out for the next installment of the series.

Author,
Alexandra Vrba